T0198622

Bram

Barbara O'Donnell

iUniverse, Inc.
New York   Bloomington

Bram

iUniverse books may be ordered through booksellers or by contacting:

*iUniverse
1663 Liberty Drive
Bloomington, IN 47403
www.iuniverse.com
1-800-Authors (1-800-288-4677)*

*Because of the dynamic nature of the Internet, any Web addresses or
links contained in this book may have changed since publication and may
no longer be valid.*

*ISBN: 978-1-4401-7309-7 (sc)
ISBN: 978-1-4401-7310-3 (ebk)*

Printed in the United States of America

iUniverse rev. date: 10/8/2009

Also by the Author

Adult novels:
Lost Soul Child
The Town
Love in an Irish Circle
Bugtown, Iowa
Dream Walker
The White Bone Harp

Children's stories:
Mary Alice
St. Francis and the Wolf
Mrs. Mumble, Bumble, Grumble
Danny Dewberry and the Bully
Eloise

Story Telling CD's:
A Christmas at St. Francis
The Black Rabbit Bar
Dooley Fagan
Memories from the Wild
So You Want to be a Writer?

Retirement Analysis and Stories: Now What?

Web site: Celticgirlswriteon.com
E-mail: Barbara@celticgirlswriteon.com

Pusheen Press
2501 W Street
Sacramento, CA 95818
(916) 454-3770

For

All those who loved Bram and especially for Kermit

~ gladly would he learn and gladly teach ~

Chaucer, the Canterbury Tales

Back row: Wim, Cor
Front row: Bram, Reit, Rudi, Hermina

Contents

Chapter 1 · Bram

I sit at my kitchen table looking at a picture of Bram. Abraham Lambrechtse. My friend. I have received notice this week of his massive stroke, brain surgery to relieve pressure, and now, five days later, his death. He was taken off life support today, doctors telling his partner and friends that there was no hope of recovery. I am immensely saddened by the news. All week I've held vigil at this kitchen table for Bram. I want him to live, to be the loving, fascinating, healthy man that I knew. I want to go to lunch and dinner with him, spend snippets of time talking to him on the phone when I need information or have a random experience or thought that I think he will enjoy. On the other hand, I do not want him to recover yet be maimed, his wonderful mind not able to function or his out-going personality able to communicate. How do I pray for Bram? What do I pray for? Well, now I know. I will pray for his spirit to find peace.

I've only known Bram for about six years, having known his partner Kermit somewhat longer. Kermit worked as a librarian at St. Francis Elementary School where I was principal. Our relationship went from employer/employee to friends over two years, and then he introduced me to Bram. I think about how the universe brings people together. I think of the unlikelihood of a European boy born in the Dutch Republic, a black boy born in Nebraska, and an Irish-

American girl born in Sacramento, but spending much time in the ancestral farmland of rural Iowa coming together some fifty years later and forming a friendship.

What did we have in common? We were of an age. We understood the history that we shared, the generational themes that we lived out. We understood each other's basic, mid-western experience, the kind of people that we grew up with, not so different whether black or white or immigrant. We talked endlessly about growing up in the 1950's, what had shaped us, what values we had inherited. We were thinking, educated folks coming from working class backgrounds. And we had chosen to be teachers, Bram and I having long careers about ready to end in retirement, Kermit, in a sense, just beginning after retirement from the State to take on the new challenge of being a children's librarian. And we had very definite views about how schools should be run and children taught.

The best thing we shared, however, was books! Bram ate up books, all kinds of books, all sizes, thicknesses, and flavors. And all that book nutrition went right to his head to long term memory where it was stored to be pulled out during all those conversations that we had. He knew everything! You couldn't bring up a subject but he couldn't carry on about, fill in the blanks, put in the details. There was hardly a philosopher, a writer, a historian that he didn't know, couldn't recommend, couldn't explain his/her most important ideas or themes. And he was a "world" reader, not specializing in American authors or British or Dutch, but he sampled and ate up Africans, Europeans, Vietnamese, Indonesians, Arabs, Greeks. Anywhere good writing and thinking was going on, Bram was definitely there.

And talk. Lord, did we talk. We talked about current events, politics, educational issues. We talked about our life experiences. We told stories on our families and friends and the characters in all those books we read. And sometimes,

Bram would get to telling stories about his life in Mattoon, Illinois, and we'd laugh our heads off! Kermit and I teased him that he sounded like Betty White's character in <u>Golden Girls</u> telling her stories about life in St. Olaf. He didn't start off to be funny, but he was… "and then Mrs. Besonhalf slipped on the ice and fell flat on her back, and somehow her voice was never the same after that." And we'd laugh ourselves hoarse.

Now Kermit and I do the talking. But hardly a discussion goes by without one of us saying, "Bram would know about that." A few weeks ago I told Kermit, "I swear you couldn't bring up any topic that Bram couldn't speak to. You could ask him why the King of Prussia wore a white ermine cape when he rode through Brussels in 1817, and you'd get an answer with a commentary." As Kermit and I talk, Bram's spirit seems to be a ghostly presence always with us.

And so I sit at my kitchen table today looking at a picture of Bram. Abraham Lambrechtse. He was an extraordinary fellow and a good friend. I want to honor his memory by writing about him, telling his story as much as I can from my perspective. I don't want to write a biography. I want to go inside my memory and write from that perspective. I want to honor the man with my words, and so I begin.

Chapter 2 - Cro-Magnon Man, Celtic Markers, Culture, and Bram

How are human beings made? What does our DNA tell us about our familial and historical selves and culture? What archetypes do our psyches carry via the genetic highway stretching backwards through time, all the way back to the first consciousness of homo sapiens? These are questions that I often debated with Bram.

Bram had his DNA traced by the National Geographic's Waitt Family Foundation. His markers first showed up in the period of Cro-Magnon man about 30,000 years ago. Bram suspected his family might have stemmed from Spain's Sephardic Jews. Abraham is a traditional name in his family, but not in Dutch history, and Lambrechtse is an unusual Dutch name. But his DNA analysis places his line clearly with Cro-Magnon roots. He was surprised he had so many Celtic markers. "I have more DNA relatives in Ireland than in Holland," he told me as he shared the report with me.

In telling Bram's story, I want to remind the reader about the basic human family story as evidenced by the study of DNA. Bram is an African, as are all of us. About 50,000 years ago, small bands of Africans began migrating north following the animal herds upon which they depended. At the time, the global ice age created a drought in Africa (the Sahara). Families began the northern trek out of Africa. Here the human family split, some making their way to Australia, and others moving north to the area of the Middle East, Central Asian steppes, India, China, and Siberia. Eventually, they crossed over to North and South America. Some continued to move west from the Asian steppes and settled in what is now modern Europe.

That's where we first find Cro-Magnon man in Southern France where the famous cave paintings of Lascaux were found in 1940. While still basically hunters/gatherers, there was a developing social hierarchy which allowed for a division of labor as elaborate stone and bone tools were made as well as jewelry, clothing, and crude shelters. There is evidence of budding agriculture. And certainly as the cave paintings indicate, art and spirituality were being established.

Cro-Magnon blended with their invaders, Celtic people, Germanic people, citizens of the Roman Empire, Vikings, and in more modern times, colonial and economic immigrants at home and abroad. Bram's family hailed from Northern, Eastern Europe, a place the Romans referred to as "the Netherlands", nether being an old English word signifying "beneath or below." The Roman civilized world considered this territory, the Netherlands, or far away, the nether part of the empire. Today we identify this region as the Netherlands, Holland, or the Dutch Republic, and the word "Dutch" seems to signify the language and culture of the region.

Turning to written history (which Bram loved to talk about), this region was part of the Roman Empire, and the Holy Roman Empire administered by Spain until 1648 when Philip IV of Spain recognized the independence of the seven northwestern provinces. Part of the southern provinces became colonies of the new country. Belgium became independent in 1830 and Luxemburg in 1980.

During the early centuries, powerful families and "kinglets" vied for territory and authority. Certain "houses" moved up or down in power and favor as was typical in most of Europe. But the House of Orange became dominant in the Netherlands, and even though the House of Orange went into exile during the Napoleonic years, it returned from England in 1813, establishing a parliamentary, democratic, constitutional monarchy. The House of Orange went into exile again during World War II, but returned to power in 1945 and remains to this day. The Dutch Republic was neutral in World War I and tried to remain so in World War II, but it was invaded by Nazi Germany in 1940.

Dutch society developed along very different lines that most of Europe. Early on, they developed a thriving middle class of businessmen, tradesmen, merchants, bankers, architects, artists, philosophers, and thinkers. By the 1700's, many people were educated, including women. During the 1700's, the Dutch became world wide tradesmen and colonists. This middle class were technically innovative, and the Dutch had a diverse economy. They developed clean, well-designed urban centers. Effective water control of rivers, marshes, and the North Sea was carried out by small, independent groups who formed notions of democratic cooperation. They had a history of independent, cooperative farmers. And the Dutch were known for establishing social justice systems in their society. They were tolerant of minorities, and much of their idealism came from their churches.

Religion was a very important aspect in shaping Dutch life. It exerted great cultural influences from the Middle Ages forward. The Dutch Roman Catholic Church fostered ideas of piety and a sober lifestyle, influencing art and business alike. During the Reformation period, a Protestant movement modeled itself after John Calvin. Protestantism flourished and became dominant in the North, while Catholicism dominated in the South. The Dutch did not form a "state" religion and freedom of conscience was generally accepted for majority and minority groups. All religions were legal and equal in status by the 19th century. Up through the 1960's, Dutch society was "pillarized," which meant that the population was segmented along religions lines. Protestants and Catholics had their own social, welfare, and school systems equally supported by the government.

Both the North and the South were colonial powers, but by the end of World War II, the North lost all her colonies except the Caribbean Islands of Aruba and Antilles. Americans might remember that it was the Dutch that colonized the Hudson Valley in the current state of New York. Indeed, the city's first European name was New Amsterdam.

Another interesting Dutch colony was present day South Africa, settled in 1652 and administered by the Dutch East India Company. Because of religions tolerance and business opportunity, many Europeans joined this colony. There were Flemish, Frisians, French Hugonauts, Germans, Scandinavians, Portuguese, Italians, Greeks, Spanish, Polish, Scots, Irish, Welsh, and English. After the second Boer War, England laid claim to the territory in 1902. Many of these "Afrikaners" chose to immigrate to other parts of Africa, especially Kenya, Argentina, Mexico, and even parts of Texas. If one had the time or energy, I'm sure you could trace Bram's DNA cousins to all parts of the world.

This is a brief, flashpoint history of Bram's culture. How do we understand Bram by understanding this culture? He came from a middle class family that valued a middle class way of life. Meaning, the family valued education, tolerance, had a clear work ethic, and loved the cultural traditions of art, literature, and especially music. Bram loved pageantry, military marching and parades, and he was especially loyal to and approved of the monarchy. Even though he eventually repudiated the Protestant Church in which he was raised, he gloried in the architecture, the ritual, and the music of the church. Christmas and other religious holidays were very important to him. He went to every Christmas concert available, singing along with the Messiah, and always buying tickets to hear Chanticleer. He decorated his house and tree, collected special ornaments of blown glass (he had over 100 of them) to hang on his tree, and regaled his friends and students with Dutch observances of Christmas complete with putting wooden shoes out on the hearth to be filled with presents by the Dutch version of Santa Claus. He strongly agreed with Christian theology regarding social justice such as the concept that we are our brother's keeper. Altogether, he had a great knowledge of his country's history, and one of his key values was that by understanding history, we can progress as human beings, not making the same mistakes again, or at least we could understand the human condition more thoroughly. The centuries of psychological development of a people were clearly evident in the personality and thinking of this particular Dutchman. And when he came to America, he brought these values with him even though he was only nine, imposing them on his understanding of his new country.

He was born in the city of Hague in 1944. And that was an auspicious time in the Dutch Republic for they had been invaded by Nazi Germany, and their government was in exile in England. It is a very significant chapter in Dutch history, and one that affects Bram and his family on a very personal level. Here's what happened.

Chapter 3 · The Nazi Years

By and large, the people of the Dutch Republic held assumptions about the uniqueness and brotherhood of man. German National Socialism repudiates this view creating a vision of a master race and hierarchy of people. The two cultures would collide. The Dutch Republic intended to remain neutral during World War II. But the Germans invaded, and after five days of fierce fighting, the Dutch capitulated on 14 May 1940. The royal family and government went into exile in England, and the die was cast. I'll tell the story of how these events affected the Lambrechtse family in the next chapter. But first I want the reader to know what happened in Bram's family's world during five years of Nazi occupation. What were the issues that shaped all of their lives? First I'll tell the macro story and then the specific mini story.

In the self interest of the Third Reich, victory over its enemies was required. In the occupied country, Dutch resources would be exploited to contribute to a German victory. At first, the Germans wanted no disturbance of peace and order to interrupt their war effort. They used the current Dutch administration, civil services, and police to administer the government. Of course, some people resigned. Parliament was dissolved, but the Nazis used conciliatory propaganda to win the Dutch people over to their side. The German troops stationed in the Republic were disciplined and tried not to disturb the residents, but by 1943, things began to change drastically.

German policy required the Germanic People as they saw the Dutch to convert whole heartedly to National Socialism and the enslavement or elimination from Europe of people antagonistic or inferior in their view. They needed this conclusion badly, but that's where their calculations fell apart. The Dutch had different, long established values that did not coincide with theirs.

> The effort to impose National Socialist concepts and institutions on Dutch society turned out to be an error because National Socialism had no historical roots in the Netherlands. The failure of this ideology to make a significant number of converts illustrates the point that "the structure of a language may make it difficult to understand – that is to make the desired responses to – concepts that have originated in another culture. Despite deceptive superficial similarities between German and Dutch culture and languages, National Socialist ideology and vocabulary were full of such concepts as the leader's principle and blood and soil theories which not only failed to elicit the desired emotional resonance but frequently provoked ridicule when attempts were made to translate them into Dutch and to transplant them into Dutch life. At the Nuremburg trials, Arthur Seyss-Inquart, Reich Commissioner for the Netherlands, admitted that the occupying power had erred in assuming that it could "form" the political will of the Dutch people and that

> authoritarian public organizations were
> superior to the voluntary ones they replaced
> (Warmbrunn 263).

Basically, the traditional loyalties such as a commitment to democracy and humanitarian principles were unshaken. Even though people were angry about parliamentary functioning being ceased, most people didn't fall for German propaganda. Of course, there were those Dutch who joined the National Socialist Party and were put into office by the Germans, but their numbers were quite small.

Until 1943, foodstuffs, goods, and fuel were at tolerable levels, but "massive exploitation" began to occur. Dutch factories worked complacently for the German war effort, and many workers were conscripted to work in Germany, or went willingly, at first, only to find themselves in horrible conditions from which they weren't free to leave. By the end of the war, the Germans were dismantling whole factories and rail lines and cars to take back to Germany. Food and fuel were conscripted as were workers. At first, large scale police or army troops were not needed to keep the peace, but by 1943, everything was changing.

At first, the attitude of the Dutch seemed to be "to keep your head down and your power dry." Many Dutch administrators and the Jewish Council believed, after some of their comrades resigned, of course, that they could do the best for their people by cooperating. They believed they were in a position to negotiate or even use passive resistance to slow down the war machine.

However, the ideological-inspired persecution of the Jews, for instance, created deep hostility toward the Germans and created large scale resistance. For many this persecution caused a violent and emotional rejection of the occupation which transcended the Jews eventually. After 1943, the arbitrary and terrorist action of the German police caused deep revulsion of the Dutch toward the regime. It was expected that police would resist the underground, a small minority of full time and part time players. But stories of brutality in factories, businesses, industry, sending people to concentration camps, and the shooting of hostages and reprisal murders enraged Dutch citizens. In April 1943, when the Germans reinstated the second labor draft, which meant that men such as Bram's father could be conscripted, the majority of the country resisted and became mobilized against the Germans.

University students were the first to speak out, especially after the dismissal of Jewish faculty members which began in 1940 but were increased by 1943. The students refused to sign the 1943 loyalty oath requested by the Nazis, and many went underground full or part time, many established newspapers. At one time there were about sixty plus small newspapers being circulated. People would read and pass along these papers which included the student's point of view regarding the war, the occupation, and news about the allies. Academic freedom had been demolished, and the student's lives were greatly affected.

The most widely influential group who spoke out about the war and rejection of Nazi values were the churches, Protestant and Catholic alike. They espoused humanitarian values and spoke to the condition of what was happening to people in general and to the Jews in particular. They continued their welfare societies to help the poor and supported their schools. The Germans were reluctant to close the churches, but many clergymen and women lost their lives, being picked off one by one.

The churches provided support for the poor, the needy, the underground, and finally the Jews. But on the Jewish question, there was no negotiation with the Nazis. As in general European culture, Dutch feelings about the Jews were ambivalent, but after 1943, the people and the churches galvanized in their attempt to save their Jewish neighbors. Still

140,000 Dutch Jews were taken away, and only about 30,000 Dutch Jews survived the war.

Organized labor was divided. Half dissolved their unions rather than negotiate with the Nazis, and others sought compromises as long as they could keep their jobs, and therefore, have money to support their families and the many benevolent societies to which they were committed. But by 1943, the unions were in open revolt and began striking. There were slow-downs, sabotage, and work refusals.

The medical communities' resistance was the most dramatic. Medical personnel refused to assist Germans in the war effort in any way, shape, or form. Their excellent organization gave support to their members, and they stuck together in their convictions. The Nazis knew that doctors and nurses were irreplaceable. Wholesale arrests and imprisonment would have been a disaster not only for the Dutch people but also for the Nazis since that act might cite the population to wholesale, active resistance.

The Jewish Council believed in reasonable cooperation with the Nazis at first. They were in no position to interfere with the war effort and some even volunteered to work at factory jobs and in labor camps thinking they could ingratiate themselves with the Germans. The Jewish Community was too secularized and fragmented to permit religious and ethnic identity to be the effective mainstay of resistance (Warmbrunn 280). Also Jews weren't persecuted because of their resistance but only because of their ethnic identity which included women and children. The threats against them were paralyzing. Since 66 A.D., Jews had lived lives of adjustment and submission, never being legal citizens in any country until the late 19th century. They as a group had no military tradition. The divisions socially with the Gentile world created another barrier to a unified resistance. And the majority of Jews lived in Amsterdam rather than rural, isolated places, so they were sitting ducks for Nazi round-ups and persecution.

How did the Dutch resist the Nazis? First, the government went into exile. Then a small underground began. As I said, an important part of underground resistance was the newspapers they wrote and circulated. By September, 1944, allied support of the underground was more active. But the biggest general resistance country-wide was the refusal of workers to go to Germany to work in the war industry after the second order was issued.

> The primary practical accomplishment of the underground movement must, therefore, be sought not so much in the actual military damage it inflicted on the enemy as in the extent to which it saved victims of Nazi persecution and deprived German factories of manpower by enabling patriots to go into hiding. But the most profound significance of the Resistance was that it helped the Dutch people to preserve with steady heart their self respect and their allegiance to common democratic and spiritual loyalties (Warmbrunn 282).

On the subject of treason, submission and reasonable collaboration to the detriment of Dutch national interests or humanitarian considerations, major figures were convicted of treason after the war. For most of the Dutch people, there was submission because they were dealing with a superior force, and resistance meant suicide. Reasonable collaboration was controversial, but those in charge thought it in the interest of the Dutch population to continue to run the government and civil service as best they could. The <u>bad news</u> was implementation of German requests by the Dutch officials. The <u>good news</u> was it kept things as normal as possible as long as possible. But eventually, the Dutch systems broke down as people were put in untenable positions and the Nazis put their own people in power.

Finally, through the persecution of the Jews and Nazification, German authorities forced a conflict with the most deep seated, patriotic, religious, moral, and ideological sentiments of the Dutch. And they lost. Here's how Bram's family was affected.

Chapter 4 · The Lambrechtse Family

Who Were the Lambrechtses? The following information and remembrances come from the children, Reit, Wim, Hermina, and Rudi (Cor is deceased). They appear to be middle class citizens living very traditional lives. Mr. Lambrechtse worked as an accountant, and Mrs. Lambrechtse was a housewife and mother. Rudi remembers his mother's father, Opa deBruin's picture where the old man is sitting in a chair, his favorite Irish Setter by his side. They lived in the city, the Hague.

Oma and Opa Lambrechtse lived in Rotterdam, where Bram's father was born and grew up. Bram's parents married in 1925 and set up housekeeping in the Hague. At some point, Oma and Opa Lambrechtse moved to the Hague and lived in an apartment building several blocks from Bram's family.

Reit remembers the "honger winter" of 1944 when she and her siblings were hustled off to her grandparents' apartment. After some hours, they were taken back home only to find their Mam in bed, and a baby, Abraham, in a bed. A visiting nurse told the children that there was "work" to be done to help their Mam. She especially recommended this to Reit, the oldest girl. Reit remembers questioning the family about his new baby, but no one considered her questions. Where had this baby come from, anyway? She says nobody talked about such things in those days. Babies just arrived.

Reit remembers her Dad and oldest brother, Cor, going to the woods outside the city to look for twigs, kindling, anything to burn for heat and cooking. This would have been dangerous as it was forbidden by the Nazis. All "fuel" went to Germany, leaving the Dutch without heat or cooking fuel in one of the coldest winters on record in Europe (1944).

Wim's wife, Rina (now deceased), told the story of a family member young wife and mother, who went to the woods with her elderly father on a similar mission to find anything at all to burn for heat and fuel. A troop of Nazi soldiers saw them, and guns drawn, shouted at them. They rushed to the man and began to interrogate him, but since he was quite deaf, he couldn't understand their questions. The young woman came to his aid and explained his deafness to the soldiers. They arrested her, letting the old man go. The family was frantic about the woman's fate, but could never have gone to the police station to ask about her. Eventually they saw a figure belly down on the street, pulling herself along with her elbows. It was the young woman who had been beaten so badly about the legs and back that she would not stand. The soldiers had released her in that condition.

During the "honger winter", Reit remembers going to centers where food was distributed. It came in high drums. Every person would get one portion. It was her duty to stand in line, waiting and waiting to get the family portion.

Bram remembered family stories about eating turnips three times a day and eventually eating tulip bulbs. Research corroborates that many people in the Dutch Republic ate their tulip bulbs that winter. Bram told other stories about people challenged to find food, hiding, a handful of grain or pats of butter down dress fronts or even in underclothing. He remembered being hungry. It wasn't until 1947, that with Allied supplies and a recovery plan, that food scarcity was lessened.

Bram had an unusual habit of taking pictures of food. When served a nice dish at a restaurant, he took a picture of it. Rudi says he once took pictures of Rudi's well-stocked refrigerator and freezer. When he came home from any trip, there amongst his pictures were photographs of food he had ordered. When I asked him about this, he replied, "You've never gone hungry, have you?" Of course, I haven't. He was only a baby up to the age of perhaps three during the hungry years, but he felt it, and what messages are rendered by family stories of famine? How important does food become in your mind?

I remember another Dutch lady that I knew some years ago. She was quite large, perhaps weighing about 300 pounds. One day, when we were talking, she said, "Have you ever wondered why I'm fat?" I was highly embarrassed because as a normal sized person, of course, I had wondered. And then she told me her story. She and her family were colonial landowners in Indonesia during the war. When the Japanese invaded, they put the family under house arrest. The family had stored food, but eventually they ran out. The lady remembers as a small girl, her grandmother had her go on her hands and knees over every inch of the store house picking any errant grain of rice that might have escaped its sack. The family trapped rats, skinned and gutted them and put them in stews. By the end of the war they were all half dead with starvation. "Yes," she said, "I have a food fetish and eat way too much, but I understand why."

In talking to the Irish about the 1845 Great Famine, one man told me the national psyche said "never again". "Even though we have plain food, we have plenty of it for everyone," he said. "We'll never go hungry again." This was in the 1970's before the Celtic Tiger roared and the whole country began to be overwhelmed with expensive restaurants and specialty grocery stores. Hunger is a powerful thing once in the family psyche.

In the National Geographic documentary, <u>Stress: Portrait of a Killer</u>, Tessa Rosebloom, a Dutch researcher, reports on a study of children in utero or born in 1944/1945, during the "honger winter." They are called the Dutch Hunger Winter Children. Rosebloom and her team followed 2,400 people to see what the consequences of famine stress played in their lives sixty plus years later. They found that these people had an adverse imprint in their brains, that their brain chemistry had been altered. They had higher levels of cardiovascular problems, higher levels of hyper cholesterol, diabetes, and psychological disorders than the general population. Their bodies had experienced incredible stress as fetuses and babies, and their bodies did not forget.

Bram had a heart attack and open heart surgery about ten years ago, type II diabetes, and of course, died of a massive stroke at the age of 64. His teeth also seemed discolored, a result of low calcium intake in early childhood.

And so the Lambrechtses survived as best they could during the terrible times as the war drew to a close. Wim remembers being trained at a moment's notice to close a square trap door in his bedroom where his father, uncle, and several other male friends would hide when the German soldiers approached their street in a "sweep" of houses to drag unwilling men off to work camps and industrial camps in Germany. The soldiers would cordon off the intersections at each end of a block and then make a house to house search for able bodied men. Luckily, the knock never came on the Lambrechtse's door. Bram remembers lingering innuendos about his father participating in the Resistance, but it was never openly discussed. In fact, Bram speculated that one of the reasons that his father wanted to immigrate was because of some unfinished business of the Resistance era that made him afraid.

Hermina tells the story of being asked by a college professor in her sophomore year to debate some World War II issues from the German position. She told him that she refused even though she was threatened with an F. At that point, she talked to her father about the Resistance and learned that he'd taken part in it. But when people go through a life or death situation, when even a small casual phrase disclosing information about your activities as an opponent of the conquering army, could mean imprisonment or death not only for yourself, but for others, possibly your family, you do not speak of certain things. And just because the war is over, how do you change those mind sets?

Reit relates that the family began talking about immigration immediately after the war. She said that she didn't want to leave, and indeed by the time the family left in 1953, she was married with a baby of her own. The family left, and she missed them terribly. She tells the story about the little boy, Bram, telling his mother that he wanted to stay with Reit as if she was putting those ideas into his head. Hermina says that it seemed their father was very concerned for his children's welfare and wanted to provide them with a much better life in the United States. It would mean a great sacrifice for him professionally, and it would mean leaving his culture and family behind, but he was determined.

And how did it come about? It all happened because of a simple comb. A girl scout troop in Mattoon, Illinois made up kits to send to "the starving children of Europe". The kits these scouts sent to Holland included soap, tooth paste and tooth brushes, and combs. When Reit's girl scout troop received the kits, everything was taken out of the kit and divided. Each girl received one thing. Reit got a comb. She was the only one that wrote a thank you note to the Illinois troop. Virginia Potter was touched to get her thank you letter. "Now," Reit said, "the children in my family can have a comb" (they must have shared one among family members prior to this gift). Virginia began writing to Reit. In a phone interview, she told me that her father was in the Rotary Club and the club encouraged the children to have world-wide pen pals. Virginia wrote to many children, but she especially loved corresponding with Reit.

Now in the town, there was a Douglas family. Judge Douglas and his wife had no children. They were Rotary members, and world travelers. And they were friends with the Potters. When they planned a European trip in 1952, Mrs. Douglas asked Virginia which of her pen pals she would like to see while in Europe, and Virginia answered right away, "Reit Lambrechtse!" Letters must have been exchanged, for when the Douglases and Potters arrived via ocean liner, the Lambrechtse family had bicycled to the landing to meet them. They were very impressed by the family and the good manners of the children. They joined the family in their home, and eventually the talk about immigration began. The Douglases offered to sponsor the family, making the 1953 move for the Lambrechtse family possible.

Hermina remembers leaving the Hague, and traveling via Rotterdam, LeHavre, Portsmouth, and arriving at the Hoboken Pier in New Jersey. Bram talked animatedly about seeing the Statue of Liberty in New York Harbor for the first time. Hermina remembers driving for two days to get to Mattoon, Illinois where the Douglas family greeted them, furnished them with a house, household goods, and gave Mr. Lambrechtse a job as a bookkeeper in a factory they owned.

They watched over the family for years, making sure that the children had scholarships to universities, even though the family got on their feet and moved to Paris, Illinois later on. They were generous people, obviously, and they had strict standards about how Americans should live. And they had prejudices also which they tried to impose on the Lambrechtses.

Strangely enough, there is another twist to this story. In January, 2009, a woman named Linda was talking to her 76 year old mother, Virginia. And for some reason her mother began telling her a story about her Dutch pen pal, the story of the comb, and how the pen pal's family had immigrated to Mattoon. Linda had never heard the story before. She googled a name that Virginia remembered, Abraham Lambrechtse. And sure enough, she found an e-mail address for him. She e-mailed, and Kermit replied and gave her Reit's and Hermina's e-mail addresses. And so there's been a reunion between Virginia and the Lambrechtses.

Bram told the story of arriving in Mattoon and walking to school with a group of neighborhood kids who happened to be black. They were just getting to know each other as the Lambrechtse children didn't speak English at this point, when Mrs. Douglas made a visit and informed the family that consorting with black people was not accepted, and if their behavior continued, they'd be turned out! Even at age nine, this outraged his sense of social justice.

What must it have felt like to leave your country where your kin had lived for 30,000 years? What did it feel like to head for an unknown place only seen through the mythology of Hollywood movies? I always found it touching when Bram spoke of seeing the Statue of Liberty, of becoming a citizen, of believing "in liberty and justice for all." "The thing is," he said, "I really believed it. I still do even though my experiences, my education provide me with no illusions about American culture and history. In some ways, I'm still that nine year old child looking at the lady in the harbor again."

Bram grew up having typical small town experiences, working for older citizens in the neighborhood, playing on a championship basketball team, and collecting up on a thousand funny stories about people in his town. He went to Washington University in St. Louis, taking a degree in political science. He often talked about being very poor while there, not having a dime in his pockets to buy a candy bar. The curriculum was extremely demanding. In literature class, for instance, they had to read a classic novel every week. In a philosophy class, they covered the entire classic Greeks in one semester. The work load was daunting. I can just imagine my Sacramento State students being asked to perform at such a level. There would be wholesale rebellion. He studied in Germany his junior year on an exchange program, and after graduating, he signed up to work for VISTA, always the idealist. After VISTA, he began his teaching career. I'll speak to those experiences in subsequent chapters.

And so Mr. Lambrechtse's wishes came true. All of his children became citizens, obtained good educations, and thrived as successful "Americans."

And finally, Rudi writes:

> My Brother and I
>
> Always bigger, always older
> Smarter, wiser, even bolder
> I was shy, not very sure
> Skinny, small, and immature
>
> Compete for grades
> Who gets the dates
> Who stays out late
> Who plays with fate
>
> Now we're friends as we have grown
> Separate lives but not alone
> Talk and share or write a letter
> Like each other all the better.

Notes on Chapter 4

After I began research for this book, I asked Bram's siblings to send me stories about their family and him. I told them not to worry about "form" but to just get their memories down that they wanted to share. I am including their e-mails and letters, in their own words, so you can get the flavor of their personalities. I've only included minor editing here and there. In order of age, here is what Wim, Reit, Hermina, and Rudi wrote to me.

Some of My Stories with Bram in our Mutual Lives
Willem

In my early years with a much younger Bram in Holland, I remember the later war years when I would jump out of our jointly occupied double bed when a sound at the door moved us into the trained procedure of closing the square hole in our bedroom floor under which our 40 year old dad (plus Uncle Tom and two billiard club friends of Dad's) were hiding in a crawl space not much higher than Bram was tall. German soldiers were going door-to-door in "razzias" to round up workers for the Reich, with machine guns placed at both sides of a particular street – in a city of near half million of stone-cold and hungry inhabitants. The knock on our door never came, fortunately; and in early May '45 our Dad rode first Cor and me on a bicycle in four days over 100 miles and under threat of aerial Allied fighter attacks to Eastern farmers who nursed us back to health in six months from extremely weakened and starvation conditions. He brought back enough food – by himself – for our Mom, four year old Hermien, one year old Bram and five months of Rudi's prenatal development (he was born 4 months later – of NORMAL weight) to survive the last two months of the "hungerwinter" before D-Day arrived. Dad in March crossed Holland again on a round trip by bicycle to get Reit into a farmer's home as well not too far from where Cor and I lived on separate farms during those six months.

I remember the early climb up Mt. Washington with Bram on an August day in 1960 after a fast dart in our shorts and gym shoes up the 4600 feet – without any water, provisions, or bad weather protection. We were scolded at the top for reckless conduct! So we bummed a ride down in an old VW bus to continue our week-long trip in my old Olds to the southern shore of the St. Lawrence mouth and tracing back along the Gaspe Peninsula, Prince Edward Island for a swim in the warm Gulf Stream, the icy cold Bay of Fundy tide swells. All this on $5 a day probably, plus cheap gas, and only one flat in Vermont! The following week our Dad dropped Rudi off at the Buffalo bus station while awaiting Bram's return by the same mode of cheap transportation. With him we "did" all of the six New England states, dropping down into gurgling mountain streams for a cooling soak and sandwich lunch "uit het vuistje" (out of your little fist!). That all took care of my first vacation while at GE's Research Lab in Schenectady.

In his college days Bram would bring Rudi along on visits East to argue into the late nights sometimes (to Rina's chagrin and admonitions to me to leave them on their own!) against my perceived corporate "surrender"! But often also good time at various friends' homes during Christmases spent East.

In more recent times I think fondly back to the first family reunion at our Mom's last birthday in 1980 when ALL six of us siblings gave Mom a birthday together that turned out to be her last one alive after all. But Bram was very instrumental in getting most of us on the West Coast when we "reunited" in both LA (overnight on the berthed Queen Mary in Long Beach) and later a few days with Kermit and Bram in their Sacramento home.

Lastly, when Rina was in remission that we celebrated in a train trip from Spain through Switzerland to Holland, I asked Bram to "do" Norway with me in a new, leased Peugeot 404 (as Rina was not up to 3000 miles of car travel to a reserved timeshare week). He flew over and we had a roaring good time driving in one day, for instance along the West Coast of Norway, up the steepest train ride in Europe and down, taking in three different ferry rides to arrive at a delta/fjord located town and hotel at the harbor's edge, where we both agreed we'd love to retire (of course, among other places in the world that we could only dream of "owning or using!). After being snowed in at our 2000 foot high timeshare resort, we split early and drove via a very Spartan but clean hotel with rented bedding and towels near Malmo, we hightailed it to Cologne in Central Germany, where Bram boarded a train for Southern Italy to see once more the early Roman settlements and supplanted/overtook the earlier Greek civilizations of 500-400 B.C.E. there. I returned to Rina in Holland before we found on her return home that her cancer had metastasized to her bones that half a year later led to her passing from us.

Because Bram had enabled us to find this Dutch doctor practicing a revolutionary anti-cancer vaccination procedure in Cologne in the summer of 2006, I invited him and his daughter Natasha (Andrew declined for personal reasons) for a two weeks vacation in Europe where after having him drive me from Amsterdam to Rome, we toured Sorrento, Pompeii and up north Venice where Natasha's best friend had just given birth to her Italian child. It was always good to have an organizing "tour guide" at your disposal (even though earlier

I had seldom needed one in doing the world with Rina!) and especially one in the family!

Kermit, that I too miss him goes without saying here, as it does not compare with your sense of grieving and severe loss of your near life-long partner and confidant! Perhaps you can see where my loss of Rina more than 26 months ago – after in essence a lifetime of having known her and really feeling her wonderfulness in my life with our "kids" for most of that time together – has induced me to share a sense of empathy with you in these harsh and painful days.

Letter from Reit

I am Reit, number two in the Lambrechtse family, the oldest daughter. Of course, I know many (things) about the family. We had before the war, a fine family, many friends, many families, many times together. We went camping in a tent on the grass floor with the farmer, a very nice family with nine children. Also, they go out with friends, Cor, me, Wim going to family or close friends, was always nice times.

It is a special way, a strange family, three kids, seven years nothing and then three kids again. Three brown eyes (our Dad), the same characters, three blue eyes (our Mam), also the same, but Hermina is in every way exactly her mother.

The family start in 1948-49 with plans going to U.S.A. From the first time I said I don't go with you, never I had an idea for leaving my country. But I was not 21 so you go, too. Till I was 21, married, getting a baby, so I stay alone from the family. It was awful, but I chosed. I like to be a nurse, so you stay home and work here. I always was working for a person. It happened so I will not look back, why??? When you look at Hermina, she had such another life, but she chosed family. They must have missed. Happened is happened. Closed. Cor, Bram, and me, yes we feeling always specials and is a good remembrance. I missed them very much…

I remember the day Bram was born. Cor, me, Wim, and Hermina must go to our grandparents, they lived a street further from our house. They took care of us. After hours, we may go back. Our Mam in bed, and baby Bram in his bed. I remember that we asked why he was in the bed, but of course, no answer. (In that time long ago, nothing was told). We had a nurse and she said "work" for the great kids, special for me.

In 1944 it starts that we start to make less food, less warming. Cold in bed. I and Mam make foot bags from parts of a blanket, so it was not too cold in bed.

Dad and Cor went to the wood to take care for a part of tree for heating and the stove. I walked to places for asking for food (cases). Then there came very high drums – with food, every person could get one portion, that was always my duty to wait on your turn to get your food. Cor, me, Wim were the last half year of the war with different farmers in eastern Holland.

After the war, it was school and help in the family. When they start in 1948 to plan to go to America, I did always say I don't go with you, but I was not 21. Bram said many times "I stay with Reit," our Mam very angry to me, but I said I didn't promise he can stay. Many times he asked it.

Four years ago he asked me, I remember that I asked it to you. I said yes you did. Cor and Bram were very closed. They tried to ask me always about the years in Holland. It is so misery that we missed so many years in the beginning they lived in U.S.A. I hope you can read and understand my letter.

Letter from Hermina

During December, I do Sinterchlass with my wooden shoes and two granddaughters… It is so hard to believe Bram is gone. Not only were we siblings but also teachers, fellow travelers, and Drum Corps nuts.

… I remember Oma and Opa Lambrechtse. They lived one block from us in the Hague in an upstairs apartment. We had family gatherings mainly at our house. Opa was with us on Sundays. I think he was a customs agent. I received a china teapot later from Oma through a younger aunt. My two names are from two Oma Lambrechtses.

Dad, Cor, and Bram had a strong family resemblance. When Bram went to Zeeland a few years back, a great uncle called out to him "Abraham" thinking he was our Dad. In Holland, Bram slept in a room with two older brothers. We played quasi-soccer in the backyard, studied in the living room, and had baths in a metal wash tub in the kitchen.

The family loved music and Moeder sang. In Illinois we had a player piano that traveled from Mattoon to Paris to Chicago. Bram and I were involved in drum corps in Illinois and later in California. Our last big drum corps trips were to Denver and the Rose Bowl in Pasadena.

I loved Bram's "black book" where he wrote down information about what he'd read, retained, and investigated.

We traveled to a number of countries together over the years. For us, a new country – Portugal. Both of us went to Italy and Spain. We used either Italian or Spanish in Portugal. We had plannings, agreements, and adventures such as the day spent at the beach at Atlantic Ocean with families we met in Lisbon. Holland has a queen. Bram went to Amsterdam when Queen Juliana abdicated and Beatrix came to the throne. For overall impact – others and family members remember his "super smarts", kindness, and caring. That's it for now. I don't want to cry too much.

Letter from Rudi

I don't recollect much about my grandparents except I have a photo of my mom's dad, Opa deBruin, sitting with his Irish Setter outside his house. My dad was born in Rotterdam, the city we left from to come to the United States. My mom was born in the Hague, the city we were born in and grew up in until we left.

We grew up in the city, where our house was across the street from a convent. Bram's encyclopedic memory came in handy when he and I visited Holland during the Christmas vacation of 1968. He led me back to the house we were born in and the current residents let us in to relive childhood memories. We took baths in a small metal tub, the youngest (me) going last.

Bram's extensive travels in Europe was again put to use when he joined Robin and me for a week in Paris, France, in February 1994. The selection of restaurants gave us a wonderful taste of French cuisine always with pictures taken of the meal before we partook.

The memory I shared at the Memorial happened during a visit that Bram and Kermit made to our house in Phoenix. Robin had put together a delightful repast, starting with a persimmon salad from our yard. Bram came into the kitchen, and on opening the well stocked refrigerator and freezer (frozen orange juice from a tree in our yard), had to take a picture.

Bram's appetite was aesthetic as well as visceral. With the richness of detail, he shared his enjoyment of life.

Chapter 5 - VISTA and Teaching Career

Bram joined VISTA (Volunteers in Service to America) in 1966, and went to Chicago for six weeks of training. He was assigned to go to Columbus, Ohio to work at a settlement house, Godman Guild, in a poor neighborhood. It has been an immigrant neighborhood where Germans, Italians, Irish, and blacks came looking for work, English classes, services for their children and themselves. I've included a historical timeline of Godman Guild and their services so you can get the idea of what they were all about. Connie Kiosse, also a VISTA volunteer who Bram met at this time, says, "I don't know who helped who the most, the poor or us. We were young, naïve, but we had large hearts and good intentions." I believe that the volunteers had a two year commitment.

We can only guess at the kind of work that they were assigned to do. Upon leaving VISTA, Bram took a teaching job in a very poor black neighborhood in Chicago. He survived very hopeless and bleak conditions for six years, but he must have left his mark on those children for thirty years later when he visited the area, at a bookstore and corner pharmacy, he ran into people that remembered him. Reading some of the comments kids here in California made upon hearing of his death, one stood out. "He made me feel like the smartest kid in the world." Another child with a stuttering problem explained, "Bram told me that the reason I stuttered was because I had so much to say…the words tripped over each other to get out. It gave me a whole new feeling about myself, a positive feeling. I slowed my speech down consciously, and that began to change my speech pattern."

After moving to Sacramento, Bram taught sixth grade at Theodore Judah and Walnutwood School before settling at Peter J. Shields Elementary in the Folsom-Cordova Unified School District where he taught third grade.

I'll never forget the story about his assignment to a learning disabled class at Theodore Judah. As he said, he knew nothing about Special Ed. as it was called in those days. He had absolutely no training in it, but because he was the latest hire on a provisional credential and had no status, he got plunked into the nightmare world of a large Special Ed. class. He had no idea what to do, but muddled through, closely observing what worked and what didn't. Of course, being Bram, and in the days before NCLB and so-called accountability, he could provide art and hands-on experience, plus music, music, music, and his children began to thrive.

However, Bram had to work on getting a California teaching credential. The State of California (stupidly, in my opinion) doesn't accept other state credentials. When he obtained his California credential, his school district changed his assignment because he wasn't licensed to teach Special Ed! Such logic boggles the mind!

Bram became very involved in the politics of schools in general and his district in particular. He believed that district and school administration needed to have policies that were fair, open, and made common sense. He found these ideals to be very lacking sometimes. We had so many talks about "the system" and how it excluded curriculum that really helped children learn. He could get very discouraged.

I have an uncle who worked in Colorado schools for thirty years who has said that all the college and institutional departments of education across the country should be burned to the ground. Their faculties, consultants, textbook writers, and staffs should be fired and never "let back into the system." The American public school system should start all over again. Then, maybe, just maybe, it would have a chance. Bram used to laugh over that and was in total agreement. It was no wonder, then, that NCLB with all its restrictions against common sense and creativity, with all it's narrowing of education, with all of its tests and measurements (of what? Bram used to say… certainly not thinking skills) almost did him in. He absolutely couldn't tolerate the system, and it couldn't tolerate him. The system wanted him to cooperate, do as he was told, embrace the new system, and he could not. He took an early retirement at age 60.

Godman Guild Historical Perspective

The first neighborhood guild association began when Ms. Anna B. Keagle, both a high school and Sunday School teacher in the Flytown neighborhood, discovered all of her 8-10 year old charges were in jail one Sunday.

In November of 1898, she and fourteen others became neighborhood activists and rented half of a brick double on West Goodale Street. By June 1899 they outgrew the house. In 1900 the Association set out to build a commodious settlement house.

Various trustees raised $6,000 to buy land and Henry C. Godman of the Godman Shoe Company gave $10,000 for the building fund. Construction began in May, 1900 and was completed in November.

Historical Highlights

1898 - The First Neighborhood Guild Association Boys' Club was established.

1900 - The First Neighborhood Guild Association became the Godman Guild Association.

Flytown was the beginning place for many immigrants coming to Columbus seeking opportunities for work and a better life. The Guild provided English classes, employment opportunities, programs and activities for boys and girls, and constant assessment of needs.

Plays, skits, music and dancing were part of the programs involving people of all ages at the Guild, especially children.

1908 - The District Nurses' Association used the Guild as a distributing point for free milk. This continued throughout the 1930's.

1910 - Supervised classes in cooking, sewing, manual training and craft work were offered and well attended at the Guild. A **1910** Guild report stated that many domestic science teachers in public schools in Cincinnati, Dayton, Findlay, Akron, Columbus and many other cities got their first practice work in the Godman Guild Domestic Science Rooms.

The Guild conducted the first supervised playground in Columbus, setting the example for the city, which began the playground movement in 1910.

The Guild pioneered the recreation center movement, which rapidly spread in the city. For many years, its gymnasium was the only one available for boys and girls at a nominal fee.

1911 - In 1910, 1,592 music lessons were given at the Guild by qualified music teachers.

1915 - The Guild's public baths were the first public baths in Columbus. Low priced baths were provided to the poor.

1917 - The Guild established community gardens located at Olentangy Boulevard at the river and West Goodale Street, north to East Third Avenue and west to the railroad, plotting seventy acres and 500 lots. Nearly 500 families raised over $20,000 in vegetables at wholesale prices in 1920. The gardens were nationally recognized in a 1930 U.S. Department of Commerce bulletin, noting its value in solving wartime food shortages and providing subsistence for the underprivileged, the unemployed and the part-time worker.

1919 - A number of groups held meetings for social and civic purposes at Godman Guild, among them, the Piave Club. O.P. Gallo, who participated in Godman Guild as a young person, suggested the name (Piave is a river in Italy) for the club. It also had a ladies auxiliary and a junior auxiliary.

Many Italians, Irish, German and African Americans felt a strong camaraderie at the guild where many developed skills for adapting to a new country.

<<image12.tif>>

1920 - With lunches packed campers boarded the train at the C.D. & M. station to go to the first Guild camp, Camp Johnson.

1921 - In cooperation with district nurses, hospitals and other health and welfare agencies, the Godman Guild provided basic human needs through baby dispensaries, prenatal care and secured material aid where necessary. Mothers and babies were sent to Camp Mary Orton for a healthful "vacation".

1922 - Organized athletic teams were character builders that not only gave the players something to do, but challenged them to be their best. William "Plunk" Ford and Murray "Chock" Ford, brothers, both played with the Harlem Globetrotters. Basketball continued until late 1950's when the gymnasium was demolished for urban renewal and freeways.

1923 - The Ohio State University College of Dentistry provided free dental care for children and adults in the Guild's service area.

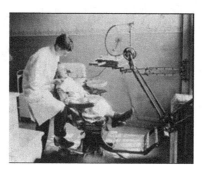

Cartoonist Billy Ireland featured the Guild's growth and service in a Columbus Dispatch illustration.

1927 - Fifty-nine miles north of Columbus, Camp Wheeler in Chesterville, Ohio, was established by Godman Guild. This camp was exclusively for African Americans.

1931 - The Guild provided excursions for individuals living in the service area. Trips included camps, athletic events, and museums.

In 1998, excursions included Niagara Falls and white water rafting.

1953 - A swimming pool was built at Camp Mary Orton.

1955 - Flytown was demolished for urban renewal and for freeway construction (I-670) in the late 1950's. Many residents moved north and continued to utilize the services of the Guild. The Guild was housed in temporary locations until 1962.

1962 - The Guild moved to 321 West Second Avenue. There were new neighbors to serve and a new service area to reshape. The neighborhood continued to feel the impacts of urban renewal, housing rehabilitation target area, commercial strip revitalization, and subsidized housing.

1965 - 1970's - The Guild was instrumental in assisting the organization of many neighborhood groups including Near Northside Neighborhood Council, Association of Near Northside Businessmen, Victorian and Italian Villages, Harrison West, Weinland Park, St. Mark's Community Health Center, Neighborhood Homes Inc., and Harper Valley Mother's Club, to name a few.

1970 - Animals were introduced to campers at Camp Mary Orton offering a good observation point to learn about nature.

1978 - Bernadine Killworth Park at the East Second Avenue office, was developed and dedicated in 1985 to honor this staff member who served the Godman Guild for forty-one years. Annual Park Pride events are held to honor volunteers.

1980 - Analysis by the Guild identified the near north side east of High Street as an area of emerging economic and social distress.

1994 - The East Sixth Avenue building became the permanent Godman Guild East Office to replace an E. Fifth Avenue storefront operation. Originally built as the Sixth Avenue Elementary School in 1961, primarily to accommodate the overflow of children in nearby local schools, the school closed in 1974. The school does not have a gymnasium/auditorium, a lunchroom or the needed space to accommodate current services and programs.

1995 - The Guild began positive alternatives to suspension from school program. It became part of the Columbus Public Schools strategic plan. Today it has evolved into the Learning Enhancement Program.

1995 - The Leadership and Challenge Center at Camp Mary Orton enables children and adults to extend their ability to achieve, lead others, and become reliable team players through ground level initiatives and high ropes courses.

1996 - A new and bigger pool was built at Camp Mary Orton with the generous contribution of Harold Squire, dedicated as the Squire Swim Center.

The Guild was designated at a National Science Foundation Math/Science Center to provide after school and in-school projects.

The Guild established its first development board to provide scholarships for neighborhood children to attend the Summer Youth Empowerment Program at Camp Mary Orton.

1998 - Year round school aged childcare programs with a learning focus were developed including Summertime Time Safari (a Summer Day Camp) and Latchkey-after-school day care.

The Guild hired its first Development Director, Mary B. Relotto.

1999 - Career Quest is a counseling program for job seekers in the community who have mental health and chemical dependency issues.

Randy Morrison celebrates 25 years as the Guild's Executive Director.

One of Ohio's most innovative employment program, Project Build, proves successful in getting under/unemployed adults training and experience in the construction industry. Eight out of eleven students completed the course and are working full time in the construction industry.

2000 - Project Build proved so successful in 1999 that the program is being offered three times during 2000. We project approximately 40 adult students will be off of welfare and working in the construction industry.

Opportunity Knocks is implemented at the Guild to work with families who will be affected during October 2000 when welfare is no longer available to them.

2001 - Godman Guild raises $1.3 million for capital improvement and additions to its 303 East Sixth Avenue location.

The community is informed that Godman Guild's 321 West Second Avenue is for sale.

2002 - The Guild holds an Open House in August celebrating the opening of the completed building at 303 East 6th Avenue.

Chapter 6 · Drum and Bugle Corps

Bram was a great devotee of the Drum Corps. He followed U.S. and International competition. He knew the rating system by which the teams were judged. He could observe a team, rate it, and come within a gnat's eyebrow of its final numbers. For three summers, he traveled with the Sacramento Free Lancers and cooked for the team. "We never ate better," team members have said.

But what is "drum corps" anyway? In 2007 when the finals were being held at Stanford University, Bram asked if I would like to attend them with him. Knowing nothing about drum corps but sensing adventure, I said yes. On a hot August afternoon, Bram, Kermit, and Jimmy, the Chinese immigrant doctor, and I headed to Palo Alto. I had no idea what to expect.

It was hot, crowded, and dusty in a grove "on the farm" where a barbeque was being feted. Bram had bought lunch tickets, of course. We stood in line for barbecued chicken, potato salad, baked beans, and all the trimmings of a very Midwestern meal. With filled plate in one hand and a cold soda in the other, we scouted for a picnic table in the shade. After we ate, Bram wandered from table to table, group to group, renewing acquaintances. He seemed to know hundreds of people.

Meanwhile, Jimmy explained to me that he had trained as a heart surgeon in China, and he explained the Chinese way of combining ancient Eastern and modern Western medical practices. Would he ever practice medicine again in this country? No, he doubted it. Even though he was studying English six hours a day at the Fremont Adult School, he realistically knew his English would never be good enough to pass the medical exams for licensure. Also, since he had not been working in the field the last few years, he would be "out of the loop" of current research. The task of preparing for licensure was overwhelming. However, he hoped to improve his English to the point where he could work in an auxiliary position in the health care industry. I had met Jimmy at a Christmas gathering a year ago at Kermit's and Bram's. I was amazed at this progress with the language in just a year. Jimmy wanted to live in this country, to have personal freedoms he couldn't have in China. Bram, with an instinct for the loneliness of the immigrant, had met him in a coffee shop and befriended him.

Bram rejoined us. "Bram, what's different about these people?" I asked, surveying the crowds around us. Mostly, it was a white, middle aged crowd, but there was something different about their clothing styles, the women's hair styles, their mannerisms. On the surface, they looked like average Americans, but on closer inspection, they were as foreign as Jimmy.

He looked about at several groups nearby that I indicated. "Oh," he chuckled, "those are East Coast people." Drum Corps was more prominent on the East Coast and Midwest. The founding headquarters was in Indiana. There was a real East Coast bias in the organization in his opinion. For instance, this was the first time the finals had been held on the West Coast since the founding of the organization in 1972.

These were classy looking people in good physical trim. Tanned men in while polo shirts and khaki pants, women with subtle make up, well groomed page boy hair cuts, starched white shirts, tan a-line skirts or slacks, expensive but not ostentatious jewelry, good sturdy expensive leather sandals and handbags, long straps over shoulders. These were prosperous looking, L.L. Bean type people, the kind that lived in affluent communities outside East Coast cities and took commuter trains to work, vacationed at resorts in the Adirondack or at upscale beach communities, Republicans, Protestants.

The Midwesterners were more given to girth, flowered blouses for the ladies, striped polos for the men, lots of polyester, and good sensible athletic shoes. Californians, few in number, stood out in jeans, T-shirts, Birkenstocks or jazzy footwear.

The crowds finished eating, stashed their garbage, and went looking for the restrooms, as the catering crew began passing out big, frosted sugar cookies. Small groups began heading for the stadium, although it was barely 4:00, and the ceremony didn't begin until 6:00. There wasn't a performer in sight, but Bram said there would be preliminary practice drills off to one side. Besides, we wanted to get a good seat, front and center. So off we trudged to the stadium.

Still I didn't know exactly what drum corps was. Bram explained. Prior to the age of radios and electronic communication, armies and navies communicated on and off the battle field with drums, fifes, and later bugles. Flag bearers were symbolic or ceremonial, but had a series of waving maneuvers which also sent out orders. After World War I when these ancient systems were becoming obsolete, veterans' organizations continued the marching drum corps tradition using brass instruments, flags, fake muskets and sabers, and of course, drums. Corp members would be taught marches of great complexity while playing the instruments and carrying the flags, muskets, and sabers.

The VFW, for instance, and many church and social organizations sponsored youth groups in particular. Drum corps is different from marching bands since they don't include reed instruments. Precision marchers in smart uniforms move onto a field and execute complicated routines while playing music.

As I watched, I remembered my church youth group leaders marching us 11-12 year olds around the church parking lot week after hot, Sacramento summer week. It was supposed to be good exercise, it would make our group learn the importance of working together, it would create internal discipline and a sense of purpose and camaraderie. In short, it was good for our souls. I remember hating it.

Clubs all over America formed, and then they began holding competitions. Hostilities broke out about the "rules" of the game. Eventually, in 1972, the Drum Corps International was founded with headquarters in Indianapolis, Indiana. This non-profit organization governed by a board of directors created policy and saw to it that the policies were carried out by their members.

The primary purpose of a DCI corps is to provide a life changing experience for youth through the art of marching music performance. Their competitive summer tour, consisting of DCI sanctioned competitions (known as the Summer Music Games) throughout the United States and Canada, culminating in August with the week-long DCI World Championships, is what these organizations build toward all summer long, to achieve the highest level of marching and music as well as color guard performance. Many other drum corps associations around the world are based upon DCI. It continues a tradition of exceptionally high-quality drum corps, with membership in the top corps highly sought after and extremely competitive, attracting the interest of potential members from many countries. (Drum Corps International)

There we sat in the Stanford stadium awaiting the performance. When the official opening of the final competition was declared and welcoming ceremonies were over, the various competing groups marched onto the field one by one, performing their much practiced maneuvers. The sound, the spectacle, the techniques were dazzling. How could these groups march, play instruments, wave flags, go through routines with saber and musket, moving forward, then in a flash, reverse, slide sideways, form abstract configurations, nip back to the original sequence and form, all the while never missing a musical beat or a single step? It was awe-inspiring, magical, and exciting. I got it! Now, I knew why this appealed to Bram, to his sense of educating children, to his Dutch sense of cooperative order, his European sense of nationalistic pride, military splendor and tradition, but more ancient, the showing off of the clan.

The finals began at 6:00 and ended at 11:30. Bram's internal mathematical calculator had ticked away during every performance, and he had told us with a few points each group's ratings. Bram's Concord, California Blue Devils took second place. The Cadets of Allen Town, Pennsylvania, won by a fraction. As we made our way out of the stadium to the parking lot, we could see drum corps groups on the sidelines packing up, parents lugging gear to busses and cars. The excitement of this final show was over. I'm afraid Kermit, Jimmy, and I didn't add much t the conversation about the event as Bram ticked off rating numbers and did a verbal analysis of the various groups' choices of music and sequence of routines, comparing each group even with the previous years' performances. How could he hold all these memories and information in his head?

I have kept the lanyard and ticket badge from the Drum Corps International, 2007. It was the last final Bram would attend. I hold that lanyard in my hands, and I remember the spectacle, the pomp and circumstance, the excitement of the competition, the thrill of the march, and music bringing tears to the eyes, a catched breath in the throat coming from some ancient memory within my bones and sinews; but most of all, I think of Bram and of all his stories about the glory and failures of the drum corps, the light in his eyes, the excitement in his voice, and ultimately, his passion for the ancient art.

Chapter 7 · Coming to Terms

What is it like to grow up gay in the United States, especially in the 1950's? Is the middle class white experience essentially different from the black, Asian, or Hispanic experience? Is the experience different in urban centers compared to rural areas? Would a child in California have a different experience than one growing up in Michigan or the Old South? These are topics for the social historians, and psychologists to ferret out. I am none of these things. I'm a writer, a reader, an observer of life.

I heard Bram's stories. I told him mine. I can emphasize, and I can sympathize, but I can never know, in a true sense, how it felt to grow up gay in his family, in his small Midwestern community. One thing that we did have in common was the times in which we grew up. It was the 1940's and early 1950's. Big bands were in decline and Elvis was coming center stage. TV became a big influence in how we thought, and how we dressed. We all remember American Band Stand, the hair, the clothing styles. And we also were aware as no past generation, that teenagers were a separate group. Our peers were becoming more important than our families. We had the convenience of cars and spending money. We had a world distinctly different from the one in which our parents grew up.

Another thing that straight and gay kids had in common was that we lived in a world of silence and repression when it came to sexuality. I can't help but wonder if Bram's experience might have been different if he had been raised in the Dutch Republic rather than the American Midwest. During this time, would there have been role models, more tolerance, more information about gays? Dr. Dan Orey took a few spoonfuls of Bram's ashes to Amsterdam this fall to scatter in the canal beside the homomonument, a monument to the homosexuals who died at the hands of the Nazis. I can't imagine any kind of monument to gays and lesbians in this country even now in 2009.

But at the age of nine, Bram was transplanted to small town Illinois. The golden rule regarding the discussion of anything of a sexual nature in our day was NEVER HAVE ONE. Nothing was openly discussed except menstruation. Well, let's face it, with blood in your panties, they had to tell you something! The middle class parents did what all good Americans do. They left "it" up to the schools.

My school sent home a permission slip for my parents to sign when I was in the sixth grade because I was about the see a Walt Disney film, a cartoon Why a permission slip to see Mickey, Minnie, and my favorite, Goofy? We girls were herded into the auditorium, and the film began. MENSTRUATION, a serious male voice said, and then continued explaining female anatomy and the menstrual cycle. The film ended with an ad for Kotex sanitary napkins. Our teacher told us where to obtain such napkins. And that was that. The boys never saw the film and would have been kept in the dark if it hadn't been for Big Mouth Brodowsky, who ran out to the playground and told the boys what we had seen. For the rest of the afternoon, Dennis Henderson sat in the back of the class making clucking noises since all us girls were apparently filled with eggs!

So how did we learn about sexuality? We observed the adults around us. From our earliest childhoods, we watched the interplay of adults and copied their behaviors. What did gay children do who had no role models? In my world, there were lots of euphemisms about sexuality... i.e. "she's p.g. again." Pregnancy was a word rarely used. "Shotgun weddings" occurred but were never explained. We observed and caught on. In our family, there was scorn heaped on women that became p.g. too often. "You should only have the number of children you can support," my grandmother told me adamantly. But she never discussed how children happened in the first place.

The second thing that formed our understanding was media. I remember I Love Lucy. She and Ricky slept in separate beds as did all TV couples. When she turned up in maternity clothes, many viewers were scandalized. Eventually, she went off to the hospital and returned with a baby, the equivalent of the "cabbage patch" or the "stork." Did the gay children get as confused as us heteros over this same business?

Then there were all those Rock Hudson/Doris Day type movies, all those titillating love scenes. Then came <u>Summer Place</u> in 1970, a steamy movie of teenage true love and make-out scenes ending up with the remorseful couple explaining Sandra Dee's pregnancy. I went to see <u>Summer Place</u> many times to ogle Troy Donohue. How did those boys feel who went to <u>Summer Place</u> to gawk at Troy Donohue? How did media inform their sexuality? How did the stories make them feel? Interesting that both movie romance hunks, Troy Donohue and Rock Hudson, were actually gay men. But we weren't to learn that for another twenty years.

In <u>Farm Boys</u>, Will Fellows describes so many gay boys from small farming, Midwestern communities who worked themselves silly in choir, church groups, 4-H, student government, school newspapers, and debate teams. Many of the interviewees said they channeled their energy into these activities to try to prove to themselves and their peer groups and families that they were worthy, young people. They describe their sexual experiences from abstinence to full intercourse and their feelings of isolation, alienation, and guilt that went along with their experiences. Most didn't begin to understand themselves or that there were other people like themselves until they left the restrictions of family, religion, and tight-knit social groups to go to college or "find work" in larger communities.

Our secretive society and certainly our religions said sex was evil outside of marriage. Then miraculously, it was ordained by God! Sexual feelings were mortal sins or the Protestant equivalent. Homosexuality didn't exist. This reminds me of Kermit's story about Franco's Spain where he lived in the 1970's. The dictator declared "there were no homosexuals living in Spain." I never heard the word gay or fag until I was in my twenties. "Queer" was considered a severe put-down, but its meaning was unclear.

My point is that we kids had no concept that we were born sexual beings, that we would grow from babies to adolescents to adults as sexual beings, and that sexuality included a whole range of behaviors. We came of age in a restrictive society who kept us in the dark, and on the other hand, titillated us via media and advertising. Ignorance, guilt, and shame were tied up with the same ribbon as all that titillation.

I don't know much about Bram's coming of age years except that he was a good student, played on a championship basketball team, and worked many odd jobs. Some of these odd jobs doing errands for old ladies are the basis for his funniest stories. I imagine he was everybody's best friend and beloved of his teachers because fifty years later, that was Bram. The budding personality doesn't change.

I know he fully came out to himself in college. I don't know about his internal struggle, but I do know that he lived in great fear of "coming out" for some time as an adult because of the homophobic society in which he lived. I know he especially feared as a teacher that he could lose his career.

And then one summer, while touring Spain, he met Kermit in Madrid. This was a real turning point in his life.

Kermit, born and raised in Omaha, had gone to college for a semester, and then went on to serve four years in the Air Force. He eventually went to L.A. and worked for the state. But by the 1970's he became disgusted with his society, as a black man and as a gay man. He decided to ditch it all and take a Yugoslavian freighter bound for Algiers. After a short adventure there (he had served at an Air Force base there prior to leaving the service), he crossed over to Spain and found work as an English teacher.

One day as he waited in line at the American Express office for news and money from home (his sister had sold his car and was supposed to wire the money to him), he noted another American in line, a distressed American since he had just been robbed on the subway. They got into a conversation, and Kermit suggested that they go back to the subway and go through the trash cans to see if they could find Bram's backpack which included his wallet and passport. They went back and did find Bram's backpack and wallet sans money.

And so began a relationship that was to last some thirty years. They spent time together in Spain, tried to establish a live-in relationship in Chicago after both returned to the U.S., and when that didn't work, mainly because of Bram's fear of being exposed, they tried a long range relationship between L.A. and Chicago. That didn't work well either. And after eight years, they agreed that they had to make a decision. Either they were going to be together in a full fledged, "out" relationship, or they were going to put the experience behind them.

Kermit didn't want to move to Chicago, and Bram didn't want to move to L.A. For both, too many ghosts abounded. It was about this time that Kermit transferred to Sacramento. It was a mutual place for both to begin again as partners. Kermit continued working for the state as a middle manager, and Bram found teaching jobs. Eventually, they bought a home in Curtis Park. Here, they established a wide circle of friends, straight and gay. When Kermit retired from state service, he took a year off, and then became the children's librarian at St. Francis Elementary, where as I have explained, I met him and eventually Bram.

By the time that I got to know Bram, he was a serious advocate for gay people and issues. He had great compassion for those who struggled whether in society, their jobs, or their families. He was very sensitive to children who experienced "otherness" whether it was a gay issue or not. He had come full circle, and he was very respected for it by everyone, straight or gay, who knew him.

Chapter 8 · Retirement Issues

By the time that Bram was sixty, the requirements, the politics, the policies detrimental to real education for children was really taking a toll on Bram's spirit. When his district announced that if forty people would sign up for early retirement, they would be granted their pension AND a golden handshake which was rather substantial. Bram was all for it. He signed up, completed the paper work, and waited to hear the outcome. And something really emerged in his psyche. Freedom! It was about to come at last. He would be free of the working life he had always known since college. He would be free of the drudgery of teaching. He would be free of the idiocy he saw in public education. He was used up, burned out; it was time to get out.

And then the bad news came. Only 37 people had signed up for the early retirement program. The deal was off. There would be no compromise, no program for the 37. Bram was devastated. As he said to me, "I can't go back to work. I've got my mind all set to leave, to retire. I just can't force myself to walk through those school doors again next August. I can't do it."

So, he took the early retirement, sans golden handshake, and sans as much income if he had waited until 65. He also had to pay for his own medical insurance, but thanks to Kaiser Permanente's Senior Care program, that only cost

$84.00/month, and at age 65 and a half, he would be eligible for Medicare. He wouldn't be eligible for social security because the school districts for which he worked were part of CALPERS. The state of California has its own system for its employees. This is common with school districts in every state. And prior part time employment, much of it paid in cash, wouldn't qualify him, of course.

He was free, and to Bram, that always meant "travel time." So he traveled frequently, a month in Brazil, Europe various times, some with his brother Wim who had purchased a new car in Europe. They toured Europe with Bram driving before shipping the car and themselves home. He went to Indonesia. He went to Palm Springs. He went and went and went. And then it all came crashing down, this freedom without adequate money to support it.

The beginning of the end from my point of view came in August of 2006 when Bram drove to southern California with the intention of picking up his sister, Hermina, and driving to Kansas to visit his very ill brother, Cor (Cor subsequently died in 2007). On the coast highway in the L.A. area, Bram drove along when a pickup pulled from a side road right out in front of him. The crash was inevitable. He was wearing his seatbelt, and the air bags in his car deployed. Bram was saved, but his car was totaled.

He made his way to a Kaiser emergency room, a motel, cancelled his trip, and took the train back home. He had to wrangle with the insurance companies for what seemed like months, and eventually, he decided not to replace his car, but to take public transportation, walk, or use the "family" car. "We're a one car family now," he told me.

And it was about this time that he said he was going back to work. "Work?" I questioned him. "Doing what?"

"Well," he said, "I signed up to substitute teach in my old district."

I tried not to act shocked. Only a year ago, when he began to talk about finding part time work and I had asked him about the notion of subbing, he had said he'd never do that. He wanted to find, perhaps a state job, something where he could do some rote job without much thinking going into it. Something to provide little structure to his life, but also to increase his income. Now, he was going back to something that he had left because of burn out, a system where he would have no say in policies or politics or outcomes. Something didn't add up.

In the next year and a half, I saw Bram increasingly talk about money concerns. I didn't want to pry. But something was wrong, something much bigger in his mind, anyway, than just a need for some pocket jingle, as we used to say in Humboldt, Iowa. During the summer after his first year of subbing, his anxiety grew. Would he get enough work this year? You could never count on exactly how much income you would have. Several applications for specialized jobs in his district had fallen through for political reasons. He even talked to me that last week in August about applying for work in a Catholic school where I had many contacts.

"Go to the Diocese website, click School Dept., and you can download their application," I told him. He did, but along with the application, came an explanation of what he would have to agree to that stopped him short. He would have to agree that he would represent the Catholic Church, although he didn't have to be a practicing Catholic. Those policies of the church were laid out clearly. And many of them were totally against his grain. How could he sign up in good faith when he disagreed with so many of these Catholic principles?

"Let me tell you," I said. "Your conscience is your guide, an informed conscience. That is Catholic doctrine. As sympathetic theologians have explained to me, since I've been in the same boat, your conscience is your conscience. However, church policy is x. As long as you understand that, and don't demonstrate against it or preach your personal beliefs in any way, shape, or form, you can work quite calmly in Catholic education. As an employee, you do represent the church and you have to act accordingly. If you can't, then don't sign up. If you are caught acting in such a way that is against church teachings, then you can be fired. It's simple."

"Gosh, I don't know what to do with this," Bram said. "I'd like to talk about it more. What I'm looking at is a steady, part time job teaching math or science to jr. high, perhaps high school level. That's it". I agreed we'd get together after Labor Day and talk some more. I'd be glad to introduce him to some of my friends/colleagues in the system so that he wouldn't get just my point of view, perhaps, the superintendent himself would grant him an occasion to talk. The super was a warm, gentle Italian man who I considered a friend. Bram said that he would like that.

But we never got the chance because the Sunday of Labor Day weekend, he had a massive stroke. Ironically, Kermit said that his e-mail was filled with requests for sub duties for the next several weeks. He would have had plenty of jobs.

Chapter 9 · The German Sisters, Esther, and a Story Born

Bram, Kermit, and I shared many stories. Bram was extremely supportive of my writing. We shared not only personal experiences, but those experiences of other people. And of course, we were great readers. All writers constantly borrow from other people whose work we read. And so, he gave me many story ideas. And here's how my story "Two Women" came about.

Bram and Kermit were good friends of two women they called the German Sisters, Karen and Ria. Both came to the United States after World War II, one as a war bride, and the other to join her sister. After some years of marriage, one sister was widowed, and the other was divorced. They lived in Kermit and Bram's neighborhood. They were immigrants, something Bram always had a soft spot for. He could speak German with them. And they were older than "the boys" and really enjoyed not only their friendship, but the help they were given. The German sisters were quite the pair, haughty, funny, and very entertaining.

When Ria had to be placed in a nursing home, her sister Karen was despondent. It wasn't long before Karen had to be located there also. Her mind was becoming more and more vague. The gentlemen managed their estate since they had no relatives in the U.S. or children to do so. The gentlemen visited the German sisters weekly, until both sisters died. This is a story that Bram told me.

Karen was lively, worldly, very bright with a challenging personality. She was wonderful to spend time with except for one thing. She was anti-Semitic. During the war, she had been a Nazi officer's mistress. He had found her work in an upscale German department store in Warsaw. She espoused his anti-Jewish sympathies entirely. He told her that if he ever called the store and told her to get on the next train to Berlin, she was to go immediately, not even returning to their apartment to get her things or even her little poodle dog. The Russians were advancing, and once they got to Warsaw, all hell was going to break loose. The day came when she got the call, and she did as she was told, and she took the last train to leave the city for some time. She tried to contact her lover, but she couldn't trace him during or after the war. Was he killed in the city, sent to the Gulag? She never found out what happened to him.

She ended up working at a military canteen in Berlin as a coffee server. And that's where she met a U.S. soldier whom she married, and they settled in Sacramento after the war. Her sister joined her and married an American. Karen talked of her war experiences and her Nazi lover and her attitude toward the Jews. Bram found this part of her personality quite taxing.

But that wasn't the end of the story. When Karen was in the nursing home, there was a little woman who adopted her. She fussed over her and reported on her condition to the gentlemen when they visited. Her name was Esther, and the gentlemen got to know her quite well. The great irony was that Esther was a Jewish woman, a survivor who posed as a Christian maid. Most of her family died during Auschwitz. And here she was taking care of a former Nazi officer's lover! "What a story!" I exclaimed hearing Bram tell it.

"You should write that one up," he encouraged. And so I did. Meanwhile, Karen died. We discussed her many times, and Bram helped me go through several drafts of the story.

One Saturday night, I sat up in bed about 3:00 a.m. and heard a voice saying, "Call Bram." I wasn't about to do it at that hour so I went back to sleep. But upon waking the next morning, I couldn't get the summons out of my mind. I waited until 9:00 a.m., and then I called. "I don't know why this voice in my head has been yelling at me since the middle of the night," I told him, "but for some reason I'm supposed to call you."

"I'll tell you why," he said. "It's Esther."

"Esther?" I asked.

"Yes, you remember Esther, the Jewish woman who took care of Karen? Well, she died a few days ago, and her obituary is in the paper today, and I'm sitting her reading it right now!" We both got the chills. "Esther is talking to you," he said matter of factly. "Would you like a copy of her obituary? It is quite a long one. She had a very interesting history. I can drop it in your mailbox tomorrow."

"Sure," I said. "I'd love to read it."

Bram made me a copy, put it in my mailbox, and indeed, it was the story of a fascinating life, but when I read the name of the daughter interviewed for the obituary, I really got the chills…Judie Panneton was the daughter. I had met Judie the previous summer when I had taken a writing/publishing class from her. She had told the class about her latest writing adventure. She was collecting stories of World War II survivors, especially death camp survivors like her mother. She was interested in their children's experiences after being born in the U.S. There was a drama, a friction, between the two generations she wanted to explore. You can say "it's a small world" or something similar, but Bram and I had a sense that it was far more than that. There was some universal connecting, some karma that was being worked out. Upon experiencing this, I got right back to working on another draft of my story. And here it is, a fictionalized account of Karen and Esther's story and the strange irony of their last days together.

TWO WOMEN

> I heard this story from a good friend who visited the woman called "Christina" in a convalescent hospital for several years before she died. I've changed the names and places of their story; however, the basic elements of the story are true. I've filled in some of the details. This is how I imagine it all happened.

An old woman sat upright, tied into a wheel chair in the day room of Bountiful Convalescent Hospital. She stared straight ahead looking at nothing. Vestiges of her past German beauty were evident, although she was ninety-five years old, with a mind as blank as a new wall.

Another woman made her way down a hallway towards the day room. She was bent and twisted with arthritis, and she moved slowly with the help of a walker. She pushed the walker ahead and shuffled her feet to catch up with it. Push, shuffle, push, shuffle. Her thin gray hair still had a streak or two of her youthful auburn and her quiet brown eyes glanced up to see how much further she had to go. It was 10:00 a.m., and the Filipina nurse had taken her roommate to the day room almost an hour ago. Nurses moved Christina around, but Anna preferred to "get her self going" each morning even if it was a slow process.

Anna reached the doorway of her room and looked about for her friend. A few people sat at card tables playing Rook or Canasta. A few more sat around a television set viewing game shows. But Anna saw Christina sitting in a corner. She stared straight ahead as if watching a movie.

Slowly, Anna made her way over to her friend. "Here you are," she said warmly. She sat down on a chair next to Christina. She reached over and took Christina's hand in hers. "How are you feeling today?" she asked kindly, but Christina did not respond. "Well, it is a beautiful day outside. Just look at those flowers," Anna said, pointing to the view from the window.

Christina slightly cut her eyes toward Anna, and then she closed them, and within minutes, her chin dropped down to her chest, and she snored softly. Anna continued to sit there looking out at the garden. It reminded her of her husband's garden. David's garden. He'd been dead over fifteen years now.

At 11:43 the little dark nurse came into the day room and announced that lunch was being served in the dining hall. In ones and twos, people moseyed out of the room and down the hall. "Christina?" Anna said, slightly shaking Christina's arm as the little nurse approached. "It's lunch time. The menu says herbed chicken, mashed potatoes, and peas. Won't that be nice? I know how you like that chicken."

The little nurse quietly unlocked the wheels of Christina's chair. Christina awakened and looked about as if she didn't know where she was, and it worried her. But Anna, now standing as best she could, balanced on the walker, trailed behind the nurse saying, "It's all right, Christina. It's all right."

The women were seated at their usual table, Christina's wheel chair being pulled up closely and Anna plumped down on a chair beside her friend. The nurse pushed Anna's walker to one side. Plates were quickly put before the women, and after closing her eyes and saying a thanksgiving prayer, Anna tucked her napkin under her chin and began to eat hungrily. But about half way through her plate of food she stopped and peered over at her friend. She had touched nothing. "Here, let me help you cut up the chicken," she said, leaning toward Christina, and with her own fork and knife she cut the chicken into bite size pieces. Next she proceeded to feed Christina, one bite at a time. But before Christina's plate was half empty, she pursed her lips tight and shook her head, as Anna encouraged her to take "one more bite." Anna sighed and laid the fork down. She was worried about how little Christina ate. It seemed that everyday, she ate less and less.

"Cookie time," a waddling, fat dumpling of a woman said coming around with a tray. "There you are, lovey," she said as Anna took three from the tray. Anna slipped one into her dress pocket to eat later in the afternoon and she began to break the others into small pieces. She repeated the food ritual. One bite for her, the other for Christina.

"Sweets for the sweet," she laughed as she pushed a nibble toward Christina's mouth. "Oooo, it's chocolate chip today. Tastes good." Christina munched down most of the cookie and smiled slightly at the tablecloth while Anna chattered about how lucky they were to have such good food and even cookies after luncheon.

A young boy came around to the tables and poured cups of tea, nodding towards the women. Anna slurped hers a little in her haste to drink it all down, but Christina's tea got cold sitting on the table. Even Anna's pleading couldn't get her to take a sip.

The Filipina nurse came over to the table and wheeled Christina back to her room. Anna reached for her walker and made her way after them. The nurse helped Christina onto her bed and tucked an afghan around her legs and feet. "There, Mrs.," she said. "You take a nap now. Good rest for you." Anna settled into a comfy chair next to Christina's bed. She held a book. "Don't read too long," the nurse said. "Rest. Rest time."

"Yes, yes," Anna said, somewhat annoyed as the nurse left the room. "Rest, rest," she mimicked to Christina. "We have lots of time to rest, but we want to find out what happens to Charlotte in this story, don't we? Now where did we leave off? Oh yes, page 72. Remember Charlotte, the young governess in the Blake household has just discovered that someone has been snooping through her dresser drawers? And she thinks it's the wicked, old housekeeper who is jealous of her?" And with that, she began to read the romance novel with much expression and delight, while her friend stared at the ceiling. And then Christina made a little snoring sound, and fell asleep.

Quietly, Anna tucked the afghan more closely around Christina, and then she sat down to continue reading, but before too long she stopped, her memories taking over, and she looked out the small window at the garden. There was something about the way the caretaker, now bending over a rose bush, moved, thrusting his head forward toward the prize plant, that unleashed memories from a long time ago. "Oh, David," she said with great emotion. "Oh, David." And all of a sudden, her memories began rolling backwards. She saw her life in reverse. She saw David smiling at her at the youth camp in Poland where she was taken after the war. She felt the fear of the concentration camp in the pit of her stomach. She saw herself on the work brigade cleaning the expensive department store. She remembered the night her family had been turned out of their home by the soldiers. She saw the walls of the university library where she studied for so many hours, and finally, she saw the beautiful dining room in her family's house where her mother lit the Sabbath candles and said the special Friday night prayers and she, as a child had been able to help the servants set the table with thick, damask linens, sparkling crystal, and heavy, engraved silverware.

On the night that the soldiers had taken her family away, they had barely had time to put on their winter coats before being shoved out into the cold night. Others on her street, playmates from her childhood, her father's business associates, old grandmothers, and young wives with crying babies made a virtual herd of people all walking east. Soldiers with guns at the ready walked behind.

Anna was frightened out of her wits. "Brave, brave," her father had admonished at his little family under his breath. "Be brave, now, brave," he said as they walked. And then Anna saw a tall, willowy, beautiful blond woman, in a luxurious fur coat and hat, clicking along in expensive high heels, her arm linked with a Nazi officer. They walked toward the herd turning to look into shop windows, chatting with each other, oblivious to the terrified herd of people in the middle of the street. The woman looked right at Anna and held her gaze for a moment, before she continued on as before, laughing a derisive, tingling laugh as the tightened her grip on her soldier.

All of a sudden there was confusion. The soldiers stopped the people. Some pointed their guns at them. Two officers argued. The talk went back and forth while the people whispered to each other. "Whatever you do, follow me," Anna's father had said quietly to his family, and as the officers argued, and a few of the soldiers put down their guns to light cigarettes and look on with disgusted faces, Anna's father saw his chance, and very calmly, he walked away from the group to the corner of a building. His wife, daughter, and two sons walked in single file after him, at first keeping closely to the building, and then cutting down alleys and running and running and running until they reached a friend's house in a distant part of the city. The friend hid them in the cellar for two weeks until it was no longer safe for his gentile family, and then Anna's family moved on, from one cellar to another, to an attic, to a servant's quarters, to the back of a shop. Moving, running, hiding.

But eventually, Anna's luck wore out. As she foraged for food at the back of a restaurant one night the cook came out of the kitchen, yelled at her, and before she could get away a waiter rushed at her and held her arm, and soon soldiers marched her away.

They took her to a cold barracks where other young women were housed and told her that she was to work on a cleaning detail with the others. The next day she was escorted by soldiers to one of the fanciest department stores in the city where she was to mop and dust, always keeping out of sight of the clientele, if possible. She began mopping in the toilets, but eventually was given a feather duster and told to keep the sparkling glass cases clean. And it was there that she saw the beautiful blonde woman again. She was leaning across a counter helping a matronly lady try on leather gloves. She was a sales woman. Anna just stood and stared at her until her supervisor gave her a shove and sent her towards the luggage department.

On another day as Anna lined up for the inventory check that was taken when her shift was over (no mop pail or feather duster was to be found missing), the beautiful blonde woman came walking past on her way out of the store. Somehow, in the hustle of other employees, she was knocked against Anna. "Oh," she said, regaining her balance. "Jew bitch!" She wiped off the side of her shoulder that had brushed against Anna as if some horrible dirt had gotten onto the sleeve of her coat.

Shortly after that Anna was sent to the camp of all horrors where she was tattooed, and there she labored doing meaningless tasks such as digging a trench only to fill it up again. Eventually, the horror, the dirt, the starvation, the sickness, the endless work, the cold made her a mechanical thing stepping through the ritual each day, not seeing, hearing, just putting one foot ahead of another, not daring to think, to cry, to laugh, or to hope. "Brave," she heard her father's voice say, but then she dared not think of her family. She dared not feel, not question, not cry out against the injustice all around her. Brave meant just putting one foot ahead of the other. That was all.

But on Friday nights, as others moaned in their sleep and tossed on their hard bunks, Anna indulged in one fantasy, one tiny thought of her life in the past, before she fell to sleep. She saw the Sabbath table and her mother lighting the candles. She repeated the prayers. "What did the words mean, after all?" she thought. But still she said them. Still she thought of the candlelight, the burning light that kept back the dark. Even in the darkness of her every moment of existence now she could remember the sparkle of that light.

And then it was over. Soldiers liberated the camp. Another truck transport, another camp, another meaningless ritual of putting one foot ahead of another. Except in this camp tiny tendrils became stalk and leaf as the good food, warm blankets, showers, and clean clothes began to bring the people back to life. And it began to happen to Anna, too.

She remembered the intense joy of holding a book in her hand, at hearing a camp boy play a violin, badly at first, but each day getting better. And then as the months went by and she began to find meaning in taking care of the younger children in the camp. And about that time David arrived.

He was an American soldier assigned to the camp, and once he spotted Anna he didn't take his eyes off her. He began bringing her small gifts, a scarf, a tin of peaches, and then they began talking about a future after the war. A future after the war! It seemed impossible. But six months later they were married by an American rabbi and David took his bride home to Berkeley, California, where, with the help of the G.I. Bill, he finished his doctorate in history.

Anna, content to decorate their small flat with things from the Salvation Army, luxuriated in fixing things up, cleaning, painting, learning how to cook, having fresh flowers on the tiny dining table, making things nice for her beloved. And on Friday nights she set the Sabbath table, lit the candles, and said the ancient prayers. She tried to trace her family but never found information about them. It was her one abiding sorrow.

A job in the Central Valley at a college brought the couple to a small bungalow near the campus. They raised three babies, all thoroughly adored by their parents, and David was a consummate gardener. Their back yard looked like an arboretum, and Anna had a house full of plants, "living sisters" as she called them.

One day as Anna stood in line at the Safeway Market to pay for her cartload of groceries she heard a Polish accent coming from the stately woman ahead of her in line. She inched closer to enjoy the sound. When the woman half turned to look at something Anna caught her breath and froze. It was the beautiful woman from Warsaw. It was the woman clinging to the arm of the Nazi officer. It was the woman that called her a Jew-bitch in the fancy department store. It was she. It was she. She backed her cart out of line carefully and when to the back of the store, where she repeated her father's words, "Brave now, brave."

At home in her own kitchen putting her groceries away, she found herself trembling with memory. Why did this woman keep coming into her life? And never in a big, significant way, in some way that would have meaning, where you could sit down with a strong cup of tea and say, "Well, yes, I see the picture now."

Many years went by. David died. Anna, crippled with arthritis, agreed with her loving children that she needed to live in a convalescent hospital. After much research, Bountiful Convalescent was chosen. It was clean, cheerful, and comfy and came highly recommended by friends who had placed a loved one there.

Anna, who appreciated rooms that were warm, clean, and cozy, settled right in to her new living arrangement. She liked the food. The Filipina staff was just like family. Her rabbi came on Saturdays for services for ten people of her faith. And even though she was twisted with her disease, she was determined to be as independent as possible, even if it took her a little longer "to get going." She liked the other residents, and she was allowed the luxury of reading in her own room to her heart's content.

One day a new gentleman was brought to the dayroom. He was a little, round man who smiled and spoke with a familiar accent. Anna sat down at the card table where he played solitaire. She reached over to shake his hand in welcome when in doing so her sweater sleeve pulled up revealing a tattoo on her inner wrist. The man stared at her wrist and then unbuttoned his shirtsleeve and drew it back showing his number, too. They sat there for a few minutes, hand outstretched to hand, looking at each other. Slowly each pulled his/her sleeve down. "Welcome, Mr. Horowitz," she said quietly.

The day came when the Filipina nurse said that Anna was getting a roommate, and an hour later, Christina was wheeled into the room. The years had altered her hauteur, but she was still the most beautiful woman Anna had ever seen. Her heart pounded as she saw the nurse arrange the woman on the bed across the room. The nurse tried to introduce them but the woman closed her eyes and didn't respond. Anna clutched at her walker and made her way down the hall to the dayroom. She felt shaken, confused. "Why is this happening?" She questioned nobody in particular.

The woman continued to ignore Anna, and Anna felt afraid. It was difficult to sleep or sit and read. It was hard to enjoy her little nest of a room. Sometimes, she felt a weight on her chest making it hard to breathe.

The weeks went by and Anna couldn't help but observe that the woman needed help. She, indeed, suffered from dementia and little by little some motherly response came upon Anna. She couldn't help but adjust Christina's wrap, help her swallow her meds, encourage her to eat. Christina began looking at Anna, really looking at her, but it was difficult for Anna to fathom what was going on in her head. And, for some reason, the more Anna did for Christina the more she wanted to do. This woman's existence had something to do with her own. That was all she knew.

More than a year went by, and one bleak, stormy night when the rain lashed down and thunder and lightning crashed outside the window, Christina awakened, and began to make small frightened noises. Anna hadn't been sleeping. She loved the intense energy of the storm, but she knew that Christina was afraid. She made her way out of bed and went to her bedside where she took the woman's hand. "There, there," she said, as if talking to one of her own babies. "It's just a crazy old storm. You're all right."

A flash of lighting hit the room, and Anna saw Christina with her head turned toward her, looking at her with blazing eyes. The vacancy of dementia was gone. "I am going to die," she said clutching Anna's hand. "I am going to die."

"Nonsense," Anna soothed. "We are all going to die someday, but tonight you're just afraid of this storm. It will be all right." She stroked her cheek, petted her hair, and then sat by the side of the bed holding her hand. Christina was breathing shallowly. And then in another flash of light, Christina looked piercingly at Anna, squeezed her hand, and said, "I'm so sorry."

Anna continued stroking Christina's hand until she knew her spirit had gone out into the storm of the night. And then she sat heavily in the bedside chair and wept for Christina.

Chapter 10 · Memories

Everybody has fond memories of Bram. Here are my two favorite stories. Bram and Kermit planned a Mother's Day brunch inviting three of us ladies. Cindy and Elizabeth had sons, but they wouldn't be spending the day with them. I had no children, but as they both said, "All those kids you either taught or administered qualify you to be a "mother." We all agreed to prepare dishes. I thought we were supposed to arrive at their house at 10:00. Cindy and I, dishes in had, arrived on time, but something was amiss.

"The drapes are drawn," I told her. "That's funny. Maybe they had to leave for a minute to go to the store." We rang the bell several times, but no one came to the door. "What should we do?" I asked. Cindy was stumped. As we stood there discussing the situation, a car pulled around the corner heading west on 4th Avenue. It was Kermit and Bram! They were heading to my house.

Their neighbor had seen us standing on the threshold, had seen them back their car out of their garage at the same time, and waved them in our direction. Bram had a covered dish on his lap and a bouquet of flowers in his hand. We all stood there in disbelief trying to figure out what happened! And then we got to laughing about our senior moment because even though we had discussed our gathering three or four times, neither Bram nor I had nailed down exactly who was hosting who? I assumed his place, and he assumed mine. It could have been a real disaster. Instead we laughed at ourselves just as Elizabeth joined us and heard our silly story. We went into THEIR house, set the table, and had a wonderful time!

And of course, there is the story of the pennies. My stepmother, who died in 1993, had saved pennies. It was a big deal with her. She even suggested that St. Francis have a penny drive to see how much money we could raise for the computer lab fund. We raised several thousand. I don't think our bank ever forgave us when we lugged in all those canvas bags of pennies! Well, at the time she was in the last stages of cancer, she told me, "When you find a penny, just think of me. I'm sending you a blessing." I had never found pennies, never looked for them.

On the morning I was flying to Iowa to attend her funeral, I had several hours to kill before the shuttle picked me up. So, I went for a walk, and when I arrived back at my door, there on the back steps was a penny. I have no doubt where it came from. From that moment on, I found pennies everywhere, at work, shopping, going for neighborhood walks, even in Ireland!

Once when walking somewhere with Bram, I found a penny and told him my story. "I'll look for them too," he said. And boy, did he find them. Every time after that when he'd get together with me, he'd have a "baggy" with pennies in it, sometimes 2 or 3, sometimes 10 or more! I began to tease him, telling him that my stepmother must like him more than me. Well, come to think of it, she was Pennsylvania Dutch.

After Bram's death, I continued to find the pennies, but I began to wonder exactly who was sending them? On so many occasions, when I was thinking of Bram, there would be a penny. For instance, my friend and I had just seen *Milk* and were hurrying out of the theatre toward the car since a light rain had begun to fall. "Bram would have loved that movie," I said to my friend. At that very moment, I avoided a puddle.

Right in the middle of it was a penny. On another day, I was going to my early morning class at CSUS, thinking about a section of Bram's story that I'd just completed, and there just inside the door of my classroom was a penny.

As I stoop to pick them up, I hear his laughter and get a glimpse of his great, big smile.

Many people wanted to add their testimony to Bram's life. I've included their thoughts, just as they wrote them.

Thirty Years of Teaching

Of course, Bram would be a teacher. In what other occupation would he have had the opportunity "to gladly learn and gladly teach" like Chaucer's scholar. As a teacher myself for forty years, I think about three-fourths of good teaching is entertaining ourselves and sharing what we know and are interested in with others, whether toddlers, retirees, or people in between. The joy of following a curriculum guide is the imaginative way you can teach the materials <u>and</u> evaluate students' knowledge and skills. Obviously, this concept doesn't occur to those people responsible for laws such as the No Child Left Behind Act, or as Bram and many other teachers called it, "the every child left behind act."

In fact, it was this current system with its rote learning and dependence on test scores that drove many imaginative teachers and especially Bram into other professions and early retirement.

It was especially interesting that a man of Bram's sophistication level would choose to teach at the elementary level. I have a theory, developed over many years of teaching and being a school principal. I think people choose a teaching level (if they have any choices at all) that mirrors their happiest learning and school experiences. For instance, my elementary school experience was good but also a muddle of experiences as my family moved a lot placing me in a new school every year, sometimes several in the same year. But in junior high, we settled for awhile, and I had a great experience at a large, urban, academically challenging school. Then we moved again, breaking my heart when I had to leave that school. High school was a boring experience. I was socially alienated from my peers and had mediocre courses of study. I never even considered going to college. That goal was never a part of my working class culture.

However, after a chance remark by a supervisor at a secretarial job I held after high school, I decided to take a few classes at my local community college. I fell in love and never looked back. As I filled out my teacher application papers for the credential program at Sacramento State University, under "level of interest" it was inevitable I would check <u>junior high</u>.

And it was inevitable that after teaching 210 junior high, very unmotivated students for two years with no help, textbooks, materials, or curriculum guides, I moved on to teaching college.

I've observed my peers over the years, and I know that my theory holds water. I suspect, then, that 3rd grade and 6th grade had been the most happy and fulfilling in Bram's life. He understood those age groups, how they thought, and how they learned. Here's a testimony from Lou Peele and Jodie Queenan, Bram's colleagues at Peter J. Shields Elementary, and Jennifer Lane with whom Bram taught at Walnutwood Elementary.

"Barbara: I spoke to several faculty here and the list started getting long. I'll do bullets and you and Kermit can pick out the best (as if all of it isn't). Here are just some of the wonderful things Bram brought to teaching:

- Taught at Peter J. Shields for 16 years. Came to the District in 1977, taught at Theodore Judah and Walnutwood before settling here. Taught 6th grade everywhere until he moved to 3rd at PJS.
- He celebrated his life with his students, having birthday cake for his birthdays, naturalization day, and the day of his arrival in the U.S. He also cooked a meal for the entire staff as his version of a birthday was sharing part of himself with everyone around. The lunches were legendary and everyone looked forward to his birthday because of it. Note: He also took several of his friends out for his birthday every

year, lately to the Mondavi Center for some type of wonderful classical music.

- Loved partner teaching and was enthusiastic about working with other teachers to provide the best possible experience for the students. Invited other teacher's classes in to celebrate. Taught singing, even though it wasn't in the curriculum so every student had some exposure to the joy of music. Brought in his DCI tapes of the finals to inspire would be musicians.

- Organized the entire school to walk down to Coloma and open their umbrellas to emulate the work of the artist Christo.

- Made sure that SEED was a program at our school (Seeking Educational Equity and Diversity), a program that many Districts now require to assist teachers in exploring their own backgrounds and stories so that they can better appreciate the stories of the students they teach.

- Teddy Bears: Bram had one of his 6th grade classes hand sew teddy bears and then give them to their buddy class.

- Bram started the system of courtesy points in PE. Attitude, not physical prowess, is rewarded during PE.

- Bram took students from his classes to a variety of places so they could experience things they never had before. He took kids to a rug store to see what they look/feel like, to concerts to hear music, and walked many of us all over downtown Sacramento to show us the art and cultures that are in our own backyard.

- He was the highlight of the end of the year party because he did the most magnificent cannon ball, and it was a challenge to survive the wave that swept through the pool.

- He started Hero's Day for Martin Luther King Jr.'s birthday at PJS wherein students would write about their heroes and then read their papers to their classes.
- He started the tradition of students making a replica of themselves and then putting them up around the multi purpose room to show how alike/different/together we were as a school.
- FCEA rep for years.
- Education for Mr. L (as he was known) was always about the experience, the seeking, the exploration of learning and not about the scores on a test. He did amazing things to bring learning to life. He brought wooden shoes from home to share his heritage with his students; showed us his papers from when his family immigrated, and had the entire 3rd grade make homemade tamales (120 of them)to bring the story "Too Many Tamales" to life for his students.
- He would celebrate the 5th of December and have students put out their shoes filled with carrots and hay to wait for Sinter Klaus. And then he would come back and fill them with treats and toys, even when he was subbing and not at that school the next day (he did this for all of the adults in SEED also).
- Teaching never stopped for Bram when the day ended. Every dinner, every trip, every staff meeting would be filled with interesting facts and discussions about the million things he knew and wanted to share."

"Bram subbed for me last Friday and I got to visit with him earlier in the week. And, a hug. The kids were pretty upset. My husband, Grant, felt that it was nice that he subbed for me on that Friday. I walked into the room on Monday and there was Bram all over. An agenda on the whiteboard. The kids had information on earth-pigs, stories of Bram's childhood, tours of Italy, and his vast knowledge of languages that they were proud to recite. And of course singing at the end of the day. I still have graded papers with his corrections on it. I was able to see him often this past year. He became a favorite at Lane and I always had the best day when my friend, Bram, came to my school site. When I called by dad on the way home, he said…"He was always a good friend to you." We did an activity today where the kids wrote their feelings and things that they wanted to remember about him. Maybe this might help with his obituary.

'He made me feel like the smartest kid in the world.'

'He made me feel special.'

'I could tell that he was going to be kind.'

'I remember looking into his eyes and into his face on that last day for the last time.' A child can only look deep into the eyes of a kind, gentle soul (I added this last sentence – Jodi).

'He was my favorite sub.'

'He taught us the meaning of the word earth-pig.'"

"Bram and I met when I first began teaching at Walnutwood Elementary in 1984. He inspired my teaching because of his personal touch with his class. Back then there were goals but teachers were allowed to create and inspire. We agreed not to talk only about the kids but talk about the world and its current affairs. He was an inspiring intellectual, someone who I needed to look up to at my young age of 30. As time went by our friendship grew stronger. We planned a trip to Europe. I would meet him in Venice, Italy, a favorite place in the world for him. After my first grueling trip on a train from Milan to Venice, being yelled at by the conductor because I had purchased the wrong ticket, I got off the train and there he was. Arms open to greet me with, "Ciao Bella!" We never stopped saying those touching words as we met and left one another. Here are some events that I will never forget. I had come down with a body rash and was one miserable girl. I told Bram that I would have to fly home at my cost because I was a mess. He marched me to the Pharmacia and told the pharmacist something and we left with a tube of salve. Within hours I was relieved and finished the trip.

Bram had bought his beloved Saab in Europe and we were making our way through Italy when we stopped at a quaint walled town to explore. Somehow my hand was caught in the window as Bram rolled it up. I screamed and then later we laughed about that for years. He took responsibility for hurting me but we knew it was my stupidity that held my hand in the window.

Another time when we were in Venice I was to meet him for lunch and I was wandering in the market and wanted to buy some fruit. Not a bushel but a couple of pieces. This led to a very angry exchange between the merchant and me. Speaking in Italian and yelling at me was more than I could take so I gave him the arm gesture that meant, up yours. Close to tears, finding Bram was like finding my sanctuary. He immediately ordered me a Grande beer and we began to exchange stories of the morning. He was always a comfort to my soul. I felt protected in a foreign land with such a knowledgeable traveler. He said he could only speak Dutch, but he always managed to get what we needed in any language. I felt safe with him. There are many memories that I have. These are just a few of the memories that we would recall to each other and laugh and laugh. I will miss his pleasant way of making me feel like a diamond. I know that my life has been enriched because of his friendship and now I will take him with me on my future adventures and I will say, "Ciao Bella!"

Khalil Gibran speaks movingly about teaching.

"Then said a teacher Speak to us of Teaching.

And he said:

No man can reveal to you aught but that which already lies half asleep in the dawning of your knowledge.

The teacher who walks in the shadow of the temple, among his followers, gives not of his wisdom but rather of his faith and his lovingness.

If he is indeed wise he does not bid you enter the house of his wisdom, but rather leads you to the threshold of your own mind.

The astronomer may speak to you of his understanding of space, but he cannot give you his understanding.

The musician may sing to you of the rhythm which is in all space, but he cannot give you the ear which arrests the rhythm nor the voice that echoes it.

And he who is versed in the science of numbers can tell of the regions of weight and measure, but he cannot conduct you thither.

For the vision of one man leads not its wings to another man.

And even as each one of you stands alone in God's knowledge, so must each one of you be alone in his knowledge of God and in his understanding of the truth."

Bram understood the "dawning of a child's knowledge." He understood the giving of his faith in the child's ability and how a lovingness of spirit brought out the child's gifts, sense of justice, and love of learning. He would gladly learn and gladly teach. That was our Bram.

Heart, Mind, Meat - Richard

It was 5:16 AM Saturday September 6, 2008 and the BPH alarm rang. It was the morning after Bram died and I stepped onto the back patio in the cool pre-dawn morning and looked up to the sky. It was still, clear, and the dark canopy was sprinkled with stars. One constellation looked like the Big Dipper.

The fact that I am astronomically challenged was clear. If I needed a lifeline to answer a million-dollar-quiz-show question, Bram would be at the top of the list. He would have pointed out the features of that pre-dawn sky and astounded me with things that I could sometimes barely understand, much less carry in my head.

The reality sunk in that Bram is gone, and the tears flowed. Bram had a generous and loving nature and was willing to find out about people and initiate conversation with anyone. His verbal skills were developed in a family environment with numerous role models. At a metaphorical level, my grief for Bram lifted, and I saw the stars in the sky as all the wonderful people I have met through him.

"We are the sum of all the people we have ever met." Part of Bram's imposing stature as a person is obviously influenced by his rich network of family, friends and colleagues.

I had the privilege of sorting through Bram's digital photos, and some of the prints from his photo albums, to prepare a Celebration of Life slide show. During this process it was clear that Bram was surrounded by a wide variety of people. It is obvious from looking at the photos.

Bram was a member of the *Boys Night Out (BNO)* group that has been meeting every Wednesday night for 22 years. Hump day became our day to punctuate the workweek, and share some male bonding. Over the years several of the members moved out of the Sacramento area, leaving a core of three: Bram, Kermit, and myself. Since Bram took his leave, now there are only two.

Bram was also a member of the *Sacramento Champagne and Social Society*, a group of like-minded persons that had also been meeting for celebratory occasions over the last 22 years. The number of gatherings has diminished as the members aged and discovered that they were looking for a comfortable place to lay down around 9 PM instead of carrying on until the wee hours of the morning.

The Champagne Society's motto: Heart, Mind, & Meat" represents three main focuses of the group: issues of the heart and passion, issues of the intellect and creativity, and issues related to the barbequed flesh (Tri Tip was a favorite).

So to honor the first fallen member of the *Champagne Society*, let's raise a glass, perform the Tri Tip Salute (it's kind of a secret) and toast Bram Lambrechtse with a vigorous "Heart, Mind and Meat."

To the memory of a man who's heart and brain were so big, that they needed a body of comparable size to support his spirit and joy of living.

Memory of Bram
Bonnie Sato/David Sato

My name is Bonnie Sato. My husband, David, passed away 8-13-08. David and Bram were teacher friends and they worked together in FCEA. Bram attended David's service of celebration and made a point to talk with me. His warm smile and genuine presence comforted me as he spoke about his relationship with David. Although I did not know Bram as well as David did, I know that he was a special person. David had become disabled at the end of his life, and it was difficult getting out. If David was still alive, the first thing he would have said upon receiving this news would have been, "We have to go to the celebration." I would have begun to make arrangements to attend. Now that David is gone and my emotions are still raw, I am not sure I will be able to be with all of you, but know that I am with you in mind and spirit. I find comfort in knowing that kindred spirits are once again united...the two of them exploring all that heaven has to offer. Knowing David, he will welcome Bram with, "You have to see this!"

This note from Donna and Nate is so indicative of messages in over 200 sympathy cards Kermit received.

"Kermit, I don't know how I can help you get through this tremendously difficult time. Bram's sudden passing is quite a great loss for us all. He is loved and missed by so many. It's difficult for me to think of you without Bram, Bram without you. Nothing can take away the fond memories. If we can do anything to help you through this don't hesitate to let us know."

This note is from Pam and Parker:

"Dear Kermit, I was so saddened when I heard about Bram. I couldn't stop thinking about how Bram always seemed to be having a good time and how he loved life and DRUM CORPS! I will always remember how both you and Bram were so kind to my grandparents (Nanny and Gramps). I know they loved you both and your kindness. I have been reading all the e-mails on the Freelancer web site and everyone mentioned how we were one of the best fed corps because of Bram and how other corps were jealous of our great meals Bram fixed. Kermit, may you find comfort in all your memories and support from family and friends. Bram was a great person and will be greatly missed. Please let us know if we can do anything."

And this note is from Liz:

"Dear Kermit, I hope Helen Keller's message will be a comfort to you eventually. I can only imagine that right now your loss is too huge and too raw for comfort of any kind.

What a shock and how unbelievable that we have lost Bram – so vibrant and so full of life! Connie is right! Bram packed much more into his life than most folks and he certainly added so much to those of us who were fortunate enough to know him.

I would like to share a couple of memories with you – one from my wedding which Bram attended in a small town in NW Ohio. While there he and my Dad got to talking and Bram spoke of a short State Route that he had traveled and referred to several landmarks along the way. My father never forgot that conversation and couldn't get over that Bram knew all about this remote little road. I kept telling my Dad that this was Bram!

My other memory is a vivid recollection of Bram soon after he met you. I believe he met you in Europe and he had returned to his place on Halsted in Chicago. I can still see him brimming with excitement and just thrilled about knowing you. I think he was a little fearful that things might not work out but this was miniscule compared to his excitement and anticipation of being with you. What a wonderful partnership you have had. I am so glad that it has been all he was so excited about those many years ago.

Kermit, please know that you are in my thoughts and prayers as you grieve. I will stay in touch."

THIS IS A BRAM ALERT!
Kermit Cain
Monday, September 1, 2008, 7:10 PM

Yesterday, Bram had a massive stroke on the left side of his brain. It was also discovered that one of his carotid arteries was completely blocked. He has problems with more than one artery in his brain. At least one clot traveled from his heart to his brain. Bram is in very critical condition.

This afternoon he is going to have a craniotomy, to open his skull to cut down the chances of the swelling on the left side of his brain pushing on his brain stem and the right side of his brain. There is no guarantee that this will work, but it's worth a try. If he survives this, he'll be on a ventilator afterwards for who knows how long. Right now he can't speak, he doesn't understand anything, and he is extremely weak on his right side.

I am extremely devastated, scared, and overwhelmed. But I had to inform all of you of this wonderful man's troubles.

Please be kind and respectful enough not to call me on the telephone or visit me for awhile because I am having a difficult time. Luckily my best friend and his daughter (my godchild) are visiting and they have helped me tremendously. Bram's sister from La Cresta Murietta, CA, is also here. One of the doctors advised me to notify the family.

Unfortunately, I do not have everyone's email address. Please pass the information on.

Thanks for understanding and I will keep you all updated.

BRAM ALERT - THE UPDATE!!!!
Monday, September 1, 2008, 9:41 PM

Hi all, Kermit is unavailable at the moment but wanted you all to know that Bram made it through the craniotomy! Bram is resting comfortable at the moment. It will be at least 5 days before we are able to tell if it was successful in regards to the swelling. On to the next battle. Please continue to send up your prayers and know that both Bram and Kermit love and appreciate you all. Thanks for your concern. Kim Goines (Kermit's Goddaughter).

BRAM UPDATE #2
Tuesday, September 2, 2008, 10:26 PM

Hello again. This is Kim again with an update on Bram's condition. Today was a very difficult day for both Bram and Kermit.

Bram had a total of 4 seizures today. The good news is that the seizures have stopped and there does not appear to be any more damage to his brain. In further good news Bram moved his right leg (in his sleep) today. This is really good because it shows that he is not completely paralyzed on the right side but may simply have some weakness. The doctors did a CT scan today and it showed that there is **NO BLEEDING** in his brain. Bram continues to be heavily medicated and unconscious. He is in ICU and is being monitored around the clock. He is still in extremely critical condition but has a great group of nurses working with him.

Kermit is doing the best that he can to be strong during this time. He is so incredibly thankful to all of you for your understanding, love, and well wishes. Please keep them coming. We are printing them out and Kermit is taking them to the hospital with him. Unfortunately, I had to return to LA today and can't physically be with them at this time. However, Kermit asked me to set up this email account so that I can keep everyone informed. Please understand that Kermit and Bram want and need all of you during this time, but Kermit just can't handle friends and family right now. He is really, really struggling. I have known Kermit all my life and I have never seen him like this. He can't bear to talk about the situation, or answer any questions right now. He is slowly coming around and I think that after this week, when there is a better idea of Bram's chances, he will be much more receptive to your generous offers of assistance. As of now he is not checking email, returning phone calls or receiving visitors. Please use this email address to contact him so that I can get your messages to him.

Thanks again for understanding and continue sending the prayers and positive energy.

BRAM AND KERMIT - BABY STEPS
Wednesday, September 3, 2008, 10:31 PM

Hi. There is really no change in Bram's condition, however, he moved **both** legs a lot more today (YEAH!). He is hanging in there and all we can do is continue to pray and wait.

Kermit on the other hand is doing much, much better and is ready to join society again. He wants, needs and would really appreciate hearing from all of you. He hasn't been able to get through all the emails (not that Kermit was ever into technology, lol), but he would like a phone call when you can. He also needs a little assistance with cooking/groceries for those of you who are local. I will let him tell you what he needs when you speak with him. He has returned to work/school so he can't really talk during the day but if you want to call him in the morning or late evening around 7 or 8 he would welcome it. Most of you know Kermit hates cell phones but he has promised to try and remember to carry it with him and turn it on.

Please keep the prayers and well wishes coming.

Thanks again, Kim.

BRAM NEWS
Thursday, September 4, 2008, 12:50 PM

At approximately 9:30 this morning Bram was given another CT scan to assess the swelling of his brain. The results were that the swelling had increased from 5 millimeters to 15 millimeters. With the increase, the left side (affected by the stroke) of the brain is now pushing on the right side as well as the brain stem. The doctors have said that it is irreversible and that Bram is very close to the criteria for being declared brain dead. His chances of recovering function are negligible or nonexistent.

Kermit is now facing the decision of removing the ventilator. The doctors feel it does not have to be done today. Taking another day will allow Kermit the chance to say goodbye. Kermit and Bram have discussed this circumstance and both have agreed that neither want to live with serious irreversible brain damage.

Kermit would like to thank all of you for your support, prayers, and well wishes. I am on my way to Sacramento and will continue to provide updates. Kim

5:45 PM
Friday, September 5, 2008, 7:38 PM

After being taken off the ventilator this morning at 8 am, Bram passed away this evening. He was surrounded by family and friends and went peacefully.

Kermit is having a "celebration" in memory of Bram's Joie De Vivre tomorrow evening (6:00) at the house. All those who are in town feel free to stop by. Bring a dish/drink and your favorite Bram story. Kermit needs all friends and family now, let's surround him with love.

Details regarding the memorial are forth coming. Kim

I can't explain how devastated I was when reviewing my email on September 1, 2008, and reading the news about Bram. I yelped as I read the first sentence. I held my breath as I read on, and then in a complete stunned almost blank state, I sat in my reading chair and stared into space for twenty minutes. I couldn't take it in. I had just seen Bram several days before, had received a nice note from him, discussing his DNA report. Bram just couldn't be stricken like the email said.

I didn't know what to pray for. I wanted him to recover, be well, yes. But I didn't want him to be "less than". And I knew Bram wouldn't want that. All I could say to God, was "This is in your hands." And then I went to the piano and played several marches. Bram loved marches, and I'd been practicing one in particular, "Marche Militaire" by Schubert, for some time hoping to get good enough to play it for Bram. I played the marches, and then the tears came flowing down my cheeks until I could no longer read the music.

Eventually, I went back to the computer and read the next news alert. I wanted to call Kermit, to be supportive, but I quite understood that he needed to be alone in his fear and sorrow. In the next few days, as I read the alerts, I began to understand all that had taken place. I had known, even in my confusion on that terrible Monday, that Bram was leaving us.

A strange thing happened on that Monday while I played the piano through my tears. It is a vivid memory. It was about 3:00 in the afternoon. All of a sudden, I heard a great "whoosh" of sound and energy. I stopped playing to look up and then around the room. The noise was gone. "That was Bram's spirit," I said aloud. In a great whoosh, it was leaving this literal life. Even though I read the alerts in the following days, something deep within, down below the areas of hope, knew that Bram had passed even though his literal body was still alive.

On Thursday, I talked to Stephanie Pierson, who said, "You have to go to the hospital to see Kermit."

"But the alerts indicated that he needed to be alone, to have his own space," I countered.

"It doesn't matter. At this point, he needs his friends around him," she said. "Just go and if you take it that he isn't up to seeing you, you'll know." I left for Sutter Hospital immediately. She was right.

I found the small waiting room where Kermit sat with his friends looking at a computer screen. I knocked, and when Kermit saw me, he got up quickly, opened the door, and gave me a great hug. "He's dying," Kermit said through tears, "Oh, he's dying." Two friends sat with him. They made room for me. I sat across the table from Kermit and held his hands as he told me about his latest conversations with the doctors. Bram was basically brain dead. The ventilator that kept his body breathing should be unplugged. Kermit didn't have to make an immediate decision. He could use some time to get used to the idea, if this is ever really possible. But within twenty-four hours, it needed to be done.

We sat talking, his friends, Kermit, and I, while Sharon Pressberg, his friend and colleague from St. Francis sat in an outer room calling friends and family on her cell phone. Finally, it was time for me to go as a few other people began to come through the door. I left Kermit and stopped in Bram's room. He lay, head bandaged, sleeping. I could hear the steady "thrum" of the ventilator. I laid my hand on his extended leg sticking out from under the bed clothes. It was very firm and cool. Patting his leg and then his arm, I told my dear friend goodbye. I told him how much he meant to me, and how I was going to miss him, and then I kissed him on the cheek, made the sign of the cross over him, and left the hospital room. Tears filled my eyes and spilled over. I could hardly find my way out of the hospital and back to the parking lot.

Kermit asked me to work with a committee of friends that would plan a memorial service for Bram which I did. And he asked me to write Bram's obituary. And here's another strange story. Several weeks before Bram died, he put an envelope in my mail box. When I opened it, it was an obituary for David Soto. Attached was a note that said he had worked with Mr. Soto, and thought him a great teacher. He really liked the way the family had written the obituary. It made Mr. Soto so human. He thought as a writer, he would share it with me. Did he have some premonition that I would use it as a model to write his own, and soon?

As soon as I began working on the first draft of the obituary I knew that I wanted to do more. I wanted to honor my friend by writing about him, by telling his story, by defining him through my perspective. Every one of his family and friends could write their own book about Bram, each person's understanding, and remembrances are slightly different. But this is my understanding of the Bram that I knew.

Kahlil Gibran in his poem <u>The Prophet</u> speaks of friendship.

"And a youth said, Speak to us of Friendship.

And he answered, saying:

Your friend is your needs answered.
He is your field which you sow with love and reap with thanksgiving.
And he is your board and your fireside.
For you come to him with your hunger, and you seek him for peace.

When your friend speaks his mind you fear not the "nay" in your own mind, nor do you withhold the "ay."

And when he is silent your heart ceases not to listen to his heart;

For without words, in friendship, all thoughts, all desires, all expectations are born and shared, with joy that is unacclaimed.

When you part from your friend, you grieve not;

For that which you love most in him may be clearer in his absence, as the mountain to the climber is clearer from the plain.

And let there be no purpose in friendship save the deepening of the spirit.

For love that seeks aught but the disclosure of its own mystery is not love but a net cast forth: and only the unprofitable is caught.

And let your best be for your friend.

If he must know the ebb of your tide, let him know its flood also.

For what is your friend that you should seek him with hours to kill?

Seek him always with hours to live.

For it is his to fill your need, but not your emptiness.

And in the sweetness of friendship let there be laughter, and sharing of pleasures.

For in the dew of little things the heart finds its morning and is refreshed.

In the sweetness of my friendship with Bram, we shared the pleasures of the mind. I will always love you, sweet, sweet Dutchman. Bon Voyage to your incredible spirit.

Works Cited

Drum Corps International. Wikipedia. 29 December 2008. 8 January 2009.

Dutch Famine of 1944. Wikipedia. 1 December 2008. 5 January 2009.

Farm Boys. ed. Will Fellows. Madison: Univ. of Wisconsin Press. 1998.

Germany. Wikipedia. 1 December 2008. 20 December 2008.

Gibran, Kahlil. The Prophet. NY: Alfred A. Knopt. 1967.

Historical Perspective of Godman Guild and Camp Mary Orton. 8 January 2009.

History of the Low Countries. eds. J.C.H. Blom and E. Lamberts. NY: Berghahn Books. 1999.

Netherlands. Wikipedia. 27 November 2008. 20 December 2009.

Seyes-Inquart, Arthur. Spartacus Educational.

Stress: Portrait of a Killer. National geographic Television and Stanford University. 2008.

Warmbrunn, Werner. The Dutch Under German Occupation, 1940-1945. Palo Alto: Stanford Univ. Press. 1963.

Works Cited Note About Wikipedia

In academic circles, Wikipedia's contents have been highly suspect in the past. As I'm new to searching encyclopedias, I googled the subject of my interest, and then clicked on everything that came onto my computer screen. That included entries by Wikipedia. And I found that when all of the information jived, as it usually did, the writing on Wikipedia was clearer and more focused than other sources. Therefore, I chose to use those cites on my works cited page.

Acknowledgements

I want to thank all those people that encouraged me to write this book, this memory of Bram. And an especial thanks to those that contributed memories of their own. I know, Lambrechtse family, that remembering your dear brother was painful at times, but I really appreciate your e-mails and letters about Bram. A big fat thanks to Janine Harrington who typed and helped edit the manuscript and to Alan Harrington for helping with layout and design.

And Kermit what can I say to you? You believed in my ability to write this book. Our mutual discussions about Bram were not only helpful to me as a writer, but to me as Bram's friend. Wherever the two of us are gathered, he is right there in the midst of us and will be forever.

Fondly,

Barbara